ESPECIALLY
JENNINGS!

Author's note

Each of the Jennings books is a
story complete in itself. Apart
from the first title, JENNINGS
GOES TO SCHOOL, the books
can be read in any order, and for
this reason I have chosen some of
the later titles for early
publication in this edition.

Anthony Buckeridge

ESPECIALLY JENNINGS!

Anthony Buckeridge

MACMILLAN CHILDREN'S BOOKS

For
JOHN HENRY AINLEY

First published 1965 by
William Collins & Sons Co. Limited

First published in this revised edition by
permission of John Goodchild Publishers.

Paperback edition, with illustrations by
Rodney Sutton, published 1988 by
MACMILLAN CHILDREN'S BOOKS
A division of Pan Macmillan Children's Books Limited
London and Basingstoke
Associated companies throughout the world

British Library Cataloguing in Publication Data
Buckeridge, Anthony, *1912*–
    Especially Jennings.
    I. Title
    823'.914[J]

ISBN 0-333-48600-5

3 5 7 9 10 8 6 4

Printed and bound in Great Britain by
Cox & Wyman Ltd, Reading, Berkshire

CONTENTS

LIST OF
ILLUSTRATIONS

Chapter 1

Flood Warning

The wash-basins in the dormitory had been filled to the brim with water. Beside the basins three boys in pyjamas stood ready to plunge their heads beneath the surface at a given signal. In the middle of the room a fourth boy was standing on a chair with hand upraised and eyes glued to the second hand of his watch.

It was a tense and solemn moment in the history of sporting contests . . . The finals of the *Dormitory Four Underwater Breath-holding Championships* were about to be decided.

"Ten seconds to zero," the starter announced in ringing tones. "On your marks! . . . Get set . . ."

The competitors by the wash-basins filled their lungs with noisy gulps of air. With straining chests and shoulders braced they awaited the word of command.

"Five . . . four . . . three . . . two . . ."

"Hey, wait a minute, Jennings. Stop the countdown! Emergency!" The interruption came from an earnest-looking eleven-year-old kneeling on a nearby bed and clutching a notebook and stub of pencil with which to record the results of the contest. "I'm not ready. My pencil's gone and busted its point."

"You shouldn't get so excited, Darbi," the starter

retorted impatiently. "Just because you're the official records-keeper, that doesn't mean to say you can . . ."

"I wasn't excited. I was just calmly chewing my pencil and listening to old Temple breathing in like a couple of vacuum-cleaners, when suddenly I noticed . . ."

From across the room came a sound like three football bladders collapsing under pressure, followed by the long-drawn sigh of a lorry applying its air brakes. . . . The competitors had run out of breath.

"Hey, Jennings! How much longer before we get started?" gasped Venables, his chest heaving and his face purple with effort. "I took in enough oxygen that time to launch a moon-rocket and now I've had to let it all go again."

"Sorry," Jennings apologised. "We had to stop the countdown because of technical trouble in the recording system. Are you ready now, Darbi?"

The official keeper of records peered at his pencil stub through the soap and toothpaste bubbles smearing the lenses of his glasses. "OK! I've just discovered there's another point at the other end."

"Right!" Jennings turned again to the gasping contestants. "Starting in five seconds from now. Stand by to draw your last breath! On your marks . . . Get set . . . Go!"

Venables, Temple and Atkinson plunged their heads down into the basins. As their faces smacked the surface of the water a tidal wave slopped over the edge and cascaded over the floor. But the finalists, intent on a record-breaking performance, were unaware of the deluge lapping the ankles of their pyjama trousers.

The chief organiser and the official records-keeper exchanged glances.

"We shouldn't have filled the basins so full," said Jennings.

"What's Old Wilkie going to say when he comes in to call silence?" queried Darbishire. "Hadn't you better stop the competition right away?"

Jennings shrugged. "Too late now. Besides, they've all got their ears under the water so they wouldn't hear, anyway."

"Yes, but what if . . .?"

"Don't panic, Darbi. They can easily mop it up with their face flannels before Sir comes round."

Jennings flashed his companion a reassuring smile. The two boys, though firm friends, were as different from each other as pepper from salt. Jennings, a few months older and half a head taller, was always eager to jump feet-first into any out-of-school activity which took his fancy, regardless of the consequences. Loyalty demanded that Darbishire – a staunch ally though never a leader – should follow his friend without question, even though he found himself involved in situations from which his law-abiding nature shrank in dismay.

Jennings glanced at his watch. Fifteen seconds had ticked away and so far none of the competitors had come up for air. It looked like being a close finish!

He had first conceived the idea of a breath-holding championship while getting undressed that evening. To begin with, he had planned it as a ruse to divert the attention of the other occupants of the dormitory so that he and Darbishire could make them apple-pie beds while their heads were under the water. But then he had been struck by the possibilities of the scheme as a sporting contest, so he had abandoned the apple-pie joke and organised a genuine competition in its place.

"It's a fantastic idea. I bet no one's ever thought of it before," he had told his friends as they were preparing for bed.

"Of course they have. I bet it's been done thousands of times," Venables had scoffed.

"Ah yes, but not seriously. Not in a big way. I bet you've never met an Olympic Gold Medallist Wash-basin Breath-holding winner, have you?"

"Well no, actually I haven't, but . . ."

"Or even a Bronze Medallist?"

"Well, no, but . . ."

"There you are then! That proves it. But if my idea gets taken up by the authorities it'll be just as popular as football or cricket in a few years' time. There'll probably be Inter-school Breath-holding matches on Saturday afternoons. Perhaps one day there'll be a Wash-basin Champion of the world; perhaps, even, of Outer Space."

Venables, Temple and Atkinson had hooted in derision. They knew Jennings' famous forecasts of old. All the same they had seized upon his suggestion as a way of enlivening a dull bedtime, and were now putting up with a great deal of discomfort and blowing a large number of bubbles in the hope of becoming champion of Dormitory Four.

At the end of twenty seconds Atkinson heaved his head out of the water and stood puffing and gasping like some astronaut who, having just landed on the moon, finds that his space-helmet has sprung a leak.

A few moments later, Temple shot up for air. The sudden jerk of his head sent more water spilling over the floor so that the area round the basins was now beginning to look like a paddling pool.

"How long was I under?" he wheezed, heedless of the

little streams running down his chest and soaking the top of his pyjama trousers.

"Twenty-four seconds," replied the organiser, glancing at his watch.

"Phew! It seemed like twenty-four hours. I wouldn't be a whale for anything."

Noises like the gurgling of a bathroom waste-pipe suggested that the third competitor was now nearing the end of his amphibious ordeal. The gurgling died away and Venables' face appeared above the waterline.

"Well done, Venables! Congratulations." Jennings thumped the winner on the back so heartily that he would have knocked the breath out of his body, had there been any breath left to knock. He seized the sagging victor's right arm and raised it aloft. "I hereby proclaim that G. Venables Esq of Linbury Court School is the new holder of the Olympic, European and Dormitory Four record for sticking his great bonce under two gallons of genuine cold tap-water for the space of twenty-nine seconds. God save the Queen!"

Venables grinned. "When do I get my gold medal?"

"Oh, *that*! Well, it so happens I'm a bit short of gold just at the moment, but . . ." Jennings broke off as he felt water oozing through his bedroom slippers. "Wow! Look at the floor! The whole room's awash! Everyone get your towels and sponges and start mopping!"

"What — me too?" complained Venables. "I'm whacked. I've just broken an Olympic record, don't forget!"

"Well, here's your chance to break another one," Jennings retorted, thrusting a bath towel into the champion's hand. "Let's see who can mop up the biggest area of flooring before Old Wilkie comes in."

Darbishire was already hard at work, using Temple's face flannel as a squeegee. "There'll be a frantic hoo-hah if he sees it like this," he prophesied. "I can't think why you blokes had to slosh it about all over the place as though you were putting a fire out."

"It was *your* job to keep the floor dry," said Atkinson. "We couldn't even breathe – let alone see what was happening."

"Don't waste time arguing. Get a move on," Jennings commanded. "Besides, there's no need to panic. Sir's still down in Dorm Two. He won't be round our way for another five minutes."

They set to work with towels, handkerchiefs, tooth-mugs and a useless scrap of blotting-paper from Darbishire's diary. But they had made little impression on the flooded flooring when Atkinson, mopping by the door, called out: "Hey, watch it! *Emergency Red!* Someone coming up the stairs."

The mopping ceased and the boys looked at one another in dismay. They hadn't a shred of excuse to cover their unlawful activities, and there was nothing they could do to conceal them.

Just like Old Wilkie! Jennings thought bitterly. What chance had a bloke got to keep one jump ahead of the duty master's movements round the building if he kept changing his routine without warning!

But when the door swung open a moment later it was not the master on duty who came into the room, but Matron, an attractive young woman in nursing sister's uniform.

The boys liked Matron. She was sensible and friendly: always ready to listen to their troubles and sometimes willing to take a tolerant view of their misdeeds.

But not *this* time! . . . Causing chaos in the dormitory was not a matter that could easily be overlooked.

"What on earth has been going on in here?" she demanded, coming to a sudden stop and surveying the scene of damp desolation before her.

Jennings flashed her a disarming smile, but switched it off again at the sight of her forbidding expression.

"Terribly sorry, Matron," he apologised. "We were just – sort of – having a friendly breath-holding competition and we never noticed the – er – the little damp patches on the floor until it was too late."

"Little damp patches!" she echoed. "That's the understatement of the year. And why in the name of reason do you have to make matters worse by soaking up the mess with your towels?"

"Well, you see, Matron, what happened was . . ."

"All right, don't bother to explain. You boys will have to watch your step." She glanced sharply at the ringleader. "Especially you, Jennings! You don't have to tell me who was responsible for *this* little upset!"

She sent Atkinson off to the broom cupboard to fetch a bucket and mops and stood frowning with annoyance as the boys repaired the damage as well as they could.

It was as well for the occupants of Dormitory Four that it was Matron rather than the master on duty who had arrived at such an untimely moment. Indeed, had their visitor been Mr Wilkins, his wrath might well have exploded with the force of a space-probe leaving its launching-pad. Matron seldom punished the boys herself, but often reported their misdemeanours to the master on duty . . . And this evening she would have plenty to report!

In the distance a heavy footstep could be heard ascending the stairs, and a moment later Mr Wilkins strode into the room to call silence and put out the light.

"Ah, hullo again, Matron!" he began jovially; and then his eye fell on the five boys with guilty expressions trying to look as though mopping the floor was a normal part of their bedtime routine.

"What's this? What's this?" he boomed. "Have these boys been giving trouble, Matron?"

The culprits crossed their fingers and waited for the blow to fall.

But, to their relief, it didn't. Matron smiled and said, "It's quite all right, Mr Wilkins. I've got the situation under control."

"But, surely, Matron, it's obvious they've been up to *something*. Wouldn't you like me to deal with them for you?"

"I'd rather you didn't," she said politely. "I can manage perfectly well, thank you."

"Yes, but . . ." It was clear that Mr Wilkins was only too anxious to step in and take charge. He was a large man with a loud voice and a short supply of patience. Though fond of the boys, he could never understand the peculiar workings of the youthful mind and always judged their behaviour from his own grown-up point of view. As a result, he seldom saw eye-to-eye with Jennings and his friends in Form Three.

Mr Wilkins shrugged. He was getting no support from Matron. "Very well then, if you prefer to cope with it yourself, there's nothing more I can do." Disappointed, he marched out of the room and shut the door with a slight bang as a sign of his annoyance.

Dormitory Four breathed again and unclasped their

crossed fingers. Good old Matron! they thought. Really good of her to stick up for us like that! . . . And when, ten minutes later, she put out the light and went downstairs, she left behind her a band of devoted admirers who would have gone to the ends of the earth to be of service to her.

"She's easily the best person on the whole staff," said Temple, speaking in a cautious whisper now that silence had been called. "Well, Matron and Mr Carter, together. I shall put them both down as tying for first place in my Top Ten favourite people for February."

"Why only February? She was just as nice last month when I was in the sick-room with my sore throat," Jennings maintained. "I was going to give her a box of chocolates or something, but I accidentally forgot about it when I got better."

"Talking of chocolates, I'll tell you another thing," Darbishire chimed in. "Sometimes when I go to the dispensary for my cough mixture she gives me . . ."

He stopped just in time. It would be asking for trouble to let everyone know that Matron kept a supply of peppermint creams in the cupboard to take away the taste of an unappetising medicine. Why, if *that* secret were to leak out there would be such a queue of wily lead-swingers with bogus coughs that there wouldn't be enough peppermint creams to go round.

Venables sat up in bed and said, "I think we ought to be specially nice to her to thank her for sticking up for us against Old Wilkie."

"How can we be nicer than we are already?" demanded Atkinson from the next bed. "Except, of course, by *not* flooding the dorm ankle-deep tomorrow night. She'd probably appreciate that."

No one had any practical suggestions to offer and the conversation drifted away to other topics. By the morning they had – with one exception – forgotten all about their good intentions of the night before.

Chapter 2

The Membership Club

The exception was Jennings. His first thought upon waking the next morning was his resolve to spread a little sunshine across the shadow of Matron's dull routine. It must be a boring job nursing mumps and chicken-pox and looking after the coughs, sore throats and chilblains of the seventy-nine boarders of Linbury Court School, he decided. Perhaps there was something he could do to lighten her load!

Five minutes after the rising bell he was washed and dressed, and urging a half-clothed Darbishire through the door with a mixture of threats and encouragement.

"What's the rush! Where are we off to?" Darbishire protested as he was chivvied along the landing at a brisk trot.

"Oh, come *on*, Darbi! You can put your sweater on going downstairs," Jennings replied impatiently. "We're going to do our good turn for Matron. Surely you haven't forgotten already."

They found Matron – an early riser – already at work in her dispensary, a large room at the far end of the first-floor landing.

"'Morning, Matron. Any odd jobs going?" Jennings

greeted her as he hurried into the room, skidded on the mat and clutched for support at a trolley-wagon piled high with delicate medical equipment.

She steered him away from the tottering bottles and rattling thermometers. "What sort of jobs?" she asked warily.

"Anything you want done," Jennings explained. "Perhaps we could help you mix up a few bottles of medicine. We'd be careful not to put in any lethal doses, honestly."

"We couldn't do much harm to that ghastly cough mixture *whatever* we put in," Darbishire said with feeling. "It tastes like diesel oil and old seaweed as it is." He glanced round in search of inspiration. "Or would you like us to give those old jars of chemicals and stuff a really good spring-cleaning?"

Matron shuddered at the generous offer of help. Apart from a couple of bulls in a china shop she could think of nothing that could do more harm in less time than the efforts of the two boys (especially Jennings) if they were let loose amongst the pharmaceutical stock in the medicine cupboard. On the other hand, she didn't want to discourage their praiseworthy attempt to be of service.

"I'm afraid there's nothing for you to do in here just at the moment," she said. "Why don't you go and ask Miss Matthews if you can help to get breakfast ready?" She felt a tinge of guilt at foisting assistance of such doubtful value upon the domestic staff, but reckoned that the boys were likely to do less damage in the kitchen than in the dispensary.

"Well, all right then, if you're quite sure," Jennings said reluctantly. "Only it was really *you* we wanted to help, not Miss Matthews."

The kitchen was bustling with activity when he and Darbishire arrived twenty minutes before breakfast was due. Miss Matthews, the cook, and her assistants were too busy frying bacon to pay much attention to offers of help, so the boys wandered through into the dining hall where Mrs Hackett, who came in daily from Linbury village, was counting out the crockery. Washing-up was Mrs Hackett's speciality and she looked upon laying the tables as something of a chore, so she was quite willing to allow them to lend a hand.

"You can put out the cornflakes while I do the side-plates," she told them. "And not too heavy-handed, mind. One packet's got to go round each table, as near as makes no difference."

Jennings took one of the twelve packets of cereals laid out on the sideboard and started to pour a generous helping on to the nearest plate. As he did so, something fell from the container with a little *plonk* and buried itself amongst the flakes. He dug with his fingers and retrieved a cheap plastic lapel badge fitted with a fastening pin on its reverse side. The letters *J.M.C.* were spaced out round the rim, enclosing a tiny picture of a space rocket in the centre. A glance at the packet in his hand revealed the explanation.

"It's New! It's Free! It's Up-to-Date!" announced the cereal carton in letters an inch high. "Join the Junior Moon Club! There's a free badge in every packet of Krunchie-Whispies! Get yours today!" In smaller type it went on: "Astronauts eat Krunchie-Whispies because they trust its body-building valuable vitamins to keep them fit on flights into space. Your Junior Moon Club badge is your passport to the Space Age. And that isn't all! It entitles you to the generous offer advertised on the reverse side of the packet, so . . ."

"Are you helping me lay the breakfast or just settling down for a nice read?" Mrs Hacket's reproving tones jolted Jennings out of the realms of space and brought him down to earth.

"Oh, sorry," he apologised, holding out the badge for her inspection. "Only, you see, I've just been appointed a Junior Moon Club astronaut."

"A *what*-onaut?" she queried.

"Astronaut. It means blokes who fly about all over the Universe," Darbishire chimed in from across the room. He, too, had found a lapel badge amongst the cereals he was dispensing and had pinned it on to his sweater. "Funny to think of people like them eating Krunchie-Whispies out in space. I always thought they had to have food out of tubes because of the way it goes floating about out of control when there isn't any gravity."

He paused to visualise a spilt carton of weightless cereals hovering in the stratosphere. There wouldn't be much crispness left in the valuable vitamins by the time they'd made a few orbits of the moon, he decided. Aloud he said, "You wouldn't be able to hear them go crunch either, would you!"

"You'll hear *me* go crunch if you don't get a move on," Mrs Hackett complained. "You've got twelve packets to dish out between you, and you haven't got properly started yet."

By the time they had finished serving the cereals, Jennings' sweater was festooned with six badges, Darbishire was wearing five, and Mrs Hackett, though somewhat over the age and weight limit for a junior astronaut, had been persuaded to pin the remaining emblem on to her overall as a symbol of her status in the Age of Space.

"Better not go into breakfast wearing all this lot or everyone will be wanting one, too," Jennings said as they left the dining hall and made their way upstairs to the common room to await the breakfast bell.

"Well, why not? We can afford to be generous," Darbishire pointed out. "We've only got to dish out the Krunchie-Whispies for a week and we'll have enough badges for everyone in the school. Or better still, we could just tell the blokes to go and help with the breakfast and get their own."

Jennings shook his head. An idea for a new project had just occurred to him – a project that depended for its success upon the source of the little badges remaining a well-kept secret.

"We don't want to let everyone get them as easily as all that," he argued. "After all, we were the first ones to find them so that makes them our own private discovery, copyright reserved. Blokes will have to come to us for them, if we don't let on where we're getting them from."

"Yes, of course. Messrs Jennings and Darbishire, *Sole Agents and Distributors*." His friend nodded approvingly and tried to look like a business tycoon planning to corner the market in industrial plastics.

"We could start a club and give all the members a free badge to prove they belonged," Jennings went on as the idea took shape in his mind. "By rights, of course, I ought to be chairman, seeing that it's my idea, and you could be secretary and honourable treasurer."

"Honorary, not honourable," Darbishire corrected. "It means I don't get paid for it."

"I should think not," Jennings retorted. "I wasn't going to have subscriptions, anyway. I was going to make it free."

The newly appointed Hon. Treasurer looked shocked. "But you *must* have subscriptions or there'll be nothing for me to take charge of. Just a small one, say five pence per person. We're bound to need money for things like – er –" He searched his mind for examples. Surely there must be *something* they could spend the money on! "Well, for things like expenses, for instance."

"Yes, of course. Expenses are bound to cost money, aren't they!"

The breakfast bell put an end to the discussion. The organisers discreetly removed the surplus badges from their sweaters and stored them in a toffee-tin in the Treasurer's locker.

"I vote we go ahead and start enrolling members straight away," Jennings observed as they hurried out on to the landing.

Darbishire nodded. "I'll make out some application forms after breakfast. We'll need everybody's full particulars: name, address, age, height, weight, telephone number. They'll have to be proposed and seconded, of course, and then we'll need another little space FOR OFFICE USE ONLY."

"What's that for?"

"So they can leave it blank. You always have it on forms when you apply for licences and things."

"Righto! I'll leave all that side of it to you."

They pattered down the stairs, eager to set their scheme in motion, and mindless of the fact that they had not yet considered the purpose for which the new venture was being formed. For both of them the immediate attraction was the choosing of members, the handing-out of badges, the filling-in of forms. These were the sort of things that gave a guy a feeling of importance . . . As for the aims and objects of the club – well, minor details like that could be discussed any old time!

At first, the boys sitting at Form Three table were too busy passing judgment on their breakfast to notice the badges which Jennings and Darbishire were wearing.

"Oh no! Not these ghastly Krunchie cereals again," groaned Atkinson as he sat down. "Sawdust and old rope – that's all it is."

From across the table Bromwich nodded in agreement. "We ought to organise a protest march. Miss Matthews might give us something different if we make a fuss."

Jennings was alarmed by the trend of these remarks. It would upset his plans completely if the housekeeper were to change to some other brand of cereal before his collection of badges was complete.

"It's really good stuff," he proclaimed, cramming a large spoonful into his mouth and champing his jaws with gusto. "Eat it up, everybody! It's bursting with body-building valuable vitamins."

Bromwich glanced at him in surprise. As a rule, Jennings was a most outspoken critic of the food provided for school meals. "You can have mine too, if you like it all that much. Whoever doled out these massive great helpings must have thought we were expecting elephants to breakfast."

Jennings ignored the reference to his open-handed generosity and turned to his friend for support. "You like it, don't you, Darbi?"

"Yes, of course. It's terrific," Darbishire agreed, switching on the bogus smile of a television advertiser. "And what's more, it's worth double. It says so on the packet."

"Worth double *what*?" Temple demanded.

"It doesn't say what. Just double. It must be true because it's the stuff that astronauts eat out in space instead of squeezing . . ." Darbishire broke off as Jennings gave him a warning nudge under the table with his knee. The less said about astronauts the better if they were to keep their secret intact.

It wasn't until the bacon and fried bread was being served that Venables noticed the lapel badges and demanded to know what they were.

"It's a club we're starting," Jennings explained, chasing a brittle fragment of fried bread round his plate with a blunt-pronged fork. "I'm Chairman and Darbishire's Hon. Sec. and treasurer."

"Annual subscription five pence per person per annum, or per part of per annum," the Treasurer added.

"What sort of a club? What do you do?" Temple asked with interest.

Jennings hesitated. "You just – sort of – belong to it. And if you're elected you get one of these badges free of charge."

"But it must be a club that *does* something," Temple persisted. "For instance, you join a football club so you can play football, or a stamp club so you can swap stamps."

"It's the same with ours, really. You join it so you can be a member."

Eyebrows were raised in puzzled wonder, but no further explanation was forthcoming.

"Well, go on," urged Venables. "What happens after that?"

"I've already told you," the Chairman replied evasively. "It's exactly the same as a football club or a stamp club, only in this case it's a membership club."

Martin-Jones, seated on Jennings' left, looked closely at the lapel badge and read out the initials printed round the rim. "*J.M.C.* What's that stand for?" he demanded.

The Chairman was taken off his guard. He had forgotten about the initials. To confess that the badge admitted the wearer to the brotherhood of the Junior Moon Club implied that his own club was sailing under false colours. Obviously, the letters must be made to stand for something else, but on the spur of the moment he had no suggestions to offer.

"Well – er – I'm not allowed to tell you," he said, playing for time. "You have to be a member before you're let into the secret."

The rest of Form Three table took this as a challenge to work out the answer for themselves.

"*J.M.C.*" Temple repeated, frowning in thought. "I bet the *J* stands for Jennings. Trust him to go and stick his own name in somewhere."

"The *C*'s bound to stand for club," Martin-Jones decided. "The Jennings *something* club."

Bromwich scowled at his fried bread and mumbled, "*M* for madmen, morons, misfits, meddlers, mischief-makers, monkey-nuts. Could stand for almost anything, couldn't it!"

It was Venables who hit upon the obvious answer. "I've got it," he cried triumphantly. "He actually told us himself. 'Everyone who joins becomes a member,' he said. It's the Jennings Membership Club."

It was as good a name as any he could think of, the

Chairman decided. They'd saved him a great deal of mental effort by providing a ready-made solution. "Yes, you're quite right," he conceded with a nod of encouragement. "Pretty smart of you to guess it so quickly."

"Don't delay. Join today!" urged Darbishire through a mouthful of bread and marmalade. "I shall deal with all applications in strict chronological order and I'm expecting a pretty big rush when the news gets around, believe me."

In this the Hon. Secretary was disappointed, for the membership drive got off to a poor start. Nobody – well, *hardly* anybody – was willing to part with five pence for the doubtful privilege of belonging to an organisation whose objectives were too vague to be described.

On the first day the only applications for enrolment came from Binns and Blotwell, the youngest boys in the school, whose only reason for joining was to obtain a badge as a symbol of equality with their elders in Form Three.

"This is hopeless," Darbishire confided to Jennings as they went to bed that evening. "I spent all morning break handing out entrance forms with *R.S.V.P.* on them, and for all the notice anyone took I might have been inviting them to a picnic in a crocodile swamp."

"Don't worry; I'll think of something," Jennings assured him. "We'll organise some exciting activities such as – er –" He searched his mind in vain for suitable suggestions. "Well, swapping matchbox tops, or something like that."

The Hon. Sec. snorted in disgust. "Matchbox tops! Call that exciting! You might as well start a club for knitting bedsocks! Honestly, Jen, you'll have to rake up some better ideas than that before you get blokes queuing up to sign on the dotted line."

Chapter 3

Something for Nothing

As it happened, Jennings found an ingenious way of aiding his recruiting drive the next morning before breakfast, when, in order to increase their stock of badges, he and Darbishire again reported to Mrs Hackett in the dining hall.

"Seventy-nine knives, forks and spoons," she said to Jennings as he trotted up to her with an obliging smile on his face. "And eight more places at the top table for masters and people. Good job you're early. I can do with a bit of help this morning."

Jennings gave the cutlery trolley a push which sent it rolling down the aisle between the tables to Darbishire at the other end of the room.

"You do the trolley, Darbi, while I dish out the corn-flakes," he commanded. "If I give everyone a really jumbo-sized helping we should get through an extra couple of packets at least."

He was so busy collecting up the little plastic badges as they tumbled on to the plates that it was not until he was serving the last table that he took any particular notice of the advertising matter on the reverse side of the packets. Then, while pouring a mountain of cereals on to Rumbelow's plate, he noticed the Special Offer.

"Free tokens for Sensational Stratosphere 'Ground to Air' Space-Gun," he read. "All holders of the Junior Moon Club badge are entitled to the free token on the lid of this packet. Three free Krunchie-Whispie tokens must be enclosed with every Space-Gun order . . ."

There were further directions in smaller type explaining how this worthwhile bargain could be obtained, and underneath was a picture of a trigger-happy Junior Moon Club astronaut peppering a distant target with deadly accuracy.

"The Krunchie-Whispie spring-loaded Stratosphere 'Ground to Air' Space-Gun fires plastic ballistic missiles a distance of sixty feet," the advertisement claimed. "The battery-operated resonator provides a life-like *Wheee-ooomph!!!* as the missile hurtles through space. Start collecting your tokens now . . ."

Jennings stopped reading and called to Darbishire. "Hey, listen! I've got something here that'll make the whole school come running to join our club. *Free Gifts!*"

"Eh!" Darbishire trundled his trolley alongside and demanded details.

"We can give every new member one of these space-guns absolutely free," Jennings explained, waving a cereal packet under his friend's nose. "All we need is three tokens for each gun. They're fantastic. They go *Wheee-ooomph!* when you fire them."

"Wow! Are you sure?"

"Well, a noise *something* like that: it says so."

"I didn't mean the noise. I meant, are you sure they're free?"

"Yes, of course – like the badges. I've just been reading all about it!" Jennings went on excitedly. "We can collect twelve coupons every breakfast-time so long as we go on helping Mrs Hackett. That'll give us four space-guns every

23

day, not counting Sundays when it's porridge and eggs."
His eyes sparkled at the prospect. "Wow! Twenty-four
guns a week. At the end of a month we could have
four times twenty-four – that's – er – sixty-four; or is it
seventy-two?"

"A hundred and forty-four," said Darbishire, guessing
wildly at the twenty-four times table.

"Four twenty-fours are ninety-six," said a deep, adult
voice from the dining-hall door. Surprised, the boys turned
to see Mr Carter standing on the threshold.

"Oh, hullo, sir. Good morning," Jennings greeted him.
"We've just had a fantastic idea. We're going to write up
for twenty-four space-guns every week and give them to
members of our membership club."

"Yes, sir. They're lethal. They go *Wheee-ooomph!* and
shoot ever so far," Darbishire added. In his excitement
he whirled the cereal packet round his head to demonstrate
the flight of a ballistic missile, and a cascade of cornflakes
floated down on to Mr Carter's head like a shower of
confetti.

"Oh, sorry, sir, I should have kept my finger on the
safety-catch," he apologised. "But you won't tell anyone
where we're getting them from, will you? We've – sort of
– cornered the market in cereals, you see, and we don't
want anyone else muscling in and spoiling it."

Mr Carter smiled as he brushed the cereals from his
hair. "I don't approve of monopolies as a rule," he said.
"But I may turn a blind eye to this one, provided it doesn't
get out of hand."

The senior assistant master at Linbury Court was a
pleasant man in his middle thirties who was liked and
respected by all the boys whom he taught. Unlike his
colleague, Mr Wilkins, he could be relied upon to take an

understanding view of what was going on in the developing minds of the ten- and eleven-year-old boys in his charge.

"The breakfast bell will be going in a few minutes," he told them. "So if you've finished helping Mrs Hackett you'd better get along and line up with the others."

Mr Carter frowned in thought as the two volunteer table-layers scampered out of the room. It was his nature to remain calm and unruffled in the face of near-disaster; but even so, the prospect of Jennings and his friends armed to the teeth with space-guns set his mind boggling with apprehension. He glanced at the illustration on the cereal packet and formed a mental picture of the common room swept by a fusillade of plastic ballistic missiles; of Matron's dispensary crowded to the doors with hopping casualties; of masters and boys leaping for cover as the dreaded *Wheee-ooomph!* sounded overhead . . . Playing with weapons of this sort was a pastime which no one (especially Jennings) should be encouraged to pursue!

Then he read the instructions in small print which Jennings, in his impulsive haste, had overlooked.

In addition to the free coupons generously provided by the manufacturers of Krunchie-Whispie cereals, it appeared that each aspiring space-gunner had also to enclose a postal order for two pounds for every weapon ordered.

Mr Carter's brow relaxed and his forebodings vanished. With a fortnight to go before half-term, the bank balances of almost all the boys were so depleted that it was doubtful whether the seventy-nine boarders of Linbury Court School could have afforded so much as a single space-gun between them. In fact, Mr Carter decided as the breakfast bell rang, there was no need for him or any other member of the staff to impose a ban when the scheme was bound to peter out of its own accord . . .

As for Jennings, it would not be fair to lay the whole blame for the misunderstanding on his shoulders. Admittedly, he should have read the small type instructions through to the end, but so many things were described as free in the misleading advertisement that he might well be pardoned for jumping to a hasty conclusion. After all, the lapel badge was free, the token was free, and the advice to take advantage of the generous offer was so freely given that, at first glance, the vexed question of two pounds was easily overlooked.

Unaware, however, of any financial stumbling block, the Chairman of the Jennings Membership Club sat down to breakfast that morning with the air of a millionaire about to distribute gifts to his less fortunate fellow-creatures.

"*Free* guns?" echoed Venables in disbelief when the offer was announced. "Free guns that shoot *sixty feet*?"

"Yes, and they're actually fitted with a battery-operated resonator," Jennings confirmed in ringing tones. "It goes *Whee-ooomph! – Whee—*" He switched off the sound effects as he caught sight of Mr Wilkins frowning at him from the top table. "Only louder than that, of course. Much louder."

"Something for nothing! Phew! I can't understand anyone doing that – especially Jennings!" said Temple. "Still, it sounds just the thing, so put me down first on the list."

"Where are you getting them from? How can you afford it?" Martin-Jones wanted to know.

The Chairman flashed him a knowing smile and winked at the Hon. Secretary. "Aha! That's our secret, isn't it, Darbi!" he said.

The offer of such a valuable free gift was too tempting to be ignored. Before breakfast was over nearly all the

boys at Form Three table had decided to join the membership club, and as the news spread other boys were quick
to follow their example. Soon after the end of morning
school the stockpile of spare badges had been exhausted
and Darbishire had to rule up a page headed *Waiting List*
in his official notebook.

By next morning when the organisers went off on their
secret mission to collect a further supply of badges and
tokens, a total of forty-nine members had been enrolled,
each of whom had been promised a Stratosphere "Ground
to Air" Space-Gun with delivery guaranteed during the
next three weeks.

"We'll wait until we've got enough coupons and then
send them all up together," the Chairman told the Secretary as they made their way into the dining hall. "I pity
the poor old postman, staggering up the drive with a
massive great parcel of forty-nine space-guns."

"Fifty-one, counting ours as well," the Secretary reminded him. "Poor old postman!"

They laughed heartily at the prospect of the staggering
postman . . . Their laughter would have been less hearty
had they realised that they had pledged themselves to give
away goods to the value of ninety-eight pounds . . .

The sudden thought that barely two weeks remained before half term occurred to Jennings in the middle of Mr
Wilkins' maths lesson a couple of days later. His parents
had already written to tell him that they would be unable
to come down to see him during the last week in February,
but had mentioned that his Aunt Angela was hoping to
celebrate the occasion by paying one of her rare visits to
the school.

Jennings gave the matter some deep thought while Mr

Wilkins' deep voice boomed away in the background about lowest common denominators and highest common factors. He must do something about Aunt Angela, he decided; she had sent him a postal order some weeks ago when he had been in the sick-room for a few days, and he had never written to thank her. That was an omission he must put right without delay, he told himself severely. There was no excuse for such discourtesy – and besides, his aunt might think twice before coming to visit a nephew who couldn't even be bothered to acknowledge a postal order.

As soon as morning school was over he took his writing pad from his desk and settled down to make amends.

"Dear Aunt Angela," he began.

"I hope you are well and having nice weather. I am well and having ditto weather as well. I think we shall have nice weather at half term as well if you can come.

"Thank you for the p.o. I did not write because I was in bed with a sore throat so I did not write but I am not in bed now as I am well, so I will write."

He frowned and scratched his nose with his pen. A mere ten lines was hardly enough to put an aunt with a genuine grievance into the right sort of mood to come down and take him out to lunch. What else could he say? . . . Oh yes, he could tell her how he'd been meaning to reward Matron's kindness to him during his brief illness by spending part of the proceeds of the postal order on a present for her. The idea had come to nothing, but it had been a generous thought on his part and would fill up a few more lines.

"Matron was kind to me when I was ill," he continued. "I was going to buy her some chocolates for being kind over my sore throat only the money got spent by mistake. We have started a membership club. You have to be a member before you can belong. We are going to have activities like space-guns and matchbox tops.

"Please come at half term as the weather will be fine and there is a good place where you can eat that I know of in Dunhambury."

He had nearly reached the bottom of the page now. Surely that was enough! Hurriedly he scrawled:

"Must stop now as my pen is leaking so can't turn over.
                              Love,
                                John."

He'd done his duty by Aunt Angela, he decided, as he sealed down the envelope. He hoped she'd realise that a nice chatty letter as long as that was well worth a good three-course lunch with ice-cream to follow.

Shortly afterwards, when he went downstairs to post his letter in the posting box, he found a number of third-formers wearing *J.M.C.* badges grouped in discussion in the hall. Rumbelow, who was holding forth at the top of his voice, broke off when he saw him descending the stairs.

"Hey, Jennings! You're going to have a riot on your hands if you don't wake your ideas up," he greeted him. "It's two whole days now since we forked out our five pences and nothing's happened yet!"

Jennings was shocked by this display of ingratitude.

"Give me a chance! I've already told you you'll have to wait for the space-guns. You'll get them all right, though, honestly!"

"Yes, but what are we supposed to do in the meantime? Pretty feeble sort of a club if we have to hang about for weeks before anything gets going." Rumbelow turned back to the discussion group. "I told you so. The whole thing's a racket. He's got no more idea of how to run a club than a left-footed sparrow."

"Yes, I have!" Jennings shouted indignantly. "Just give me a few days and I'll prove it."

Even so, it was almost a week later and the morale of the members was at a low ebb before an idea for a worthwhile activity occurred to him.

The Easter term was producing its usual crop of minor ailments, and on Monday Venables retired to the sick-room with a bilious attack. He reappeared on Saturday, restored to health, and clutching a dusty cardboard box containing an ancient partly-dismantled radio and a pair of earphones.

"Look what I found in a cupboard in the sick-room," he said to Temple and Atkinson who were reading in the common room after football practice. "Matron says it's an old one people used to have years and years ago. She'd forgotten about it till I discovered it under a stack of ancient annuals."

"I bet it doesn't work," said Temple, sauntering across the room to inspect the discovery at close quarters.

"Matron says it *did* work the last time they tried it." Venables dived into the box and started laying the components out on the common-room table. "Mind you, that was about a thousand years ago when Marconi was still trying to send Morse across the Atlantic. But we could put it together and see, couldn't we! Matron would have thrown it out if I hadn't stopped her."

Atkinson abandoned his book and the three boys set about sorting out and examining the old-fashioned equipment.

So far as they could tell, the apparatus was complete; and when, ten minutes later, Jennings and Darbishire came into the room, Venables and Temple were busy fiddling with the controls while Atkinson, wearing the ill-fitting earphones, was trying to uncoil a cat's-cradle of tangled wire.

"Antique scientific salvage," Venables announced proudly. "Fantastic, isn't it!"

Darbishire peered doubtfully at the cracked terminals and wobbly knobs.

"Looks like William the Conqueror's walkie-talkie at the Battle of Hastings," he decided. "I've never seen a radio like this before."

"It's an old crystal set," said Temple. "No valves, no transistors. Just twiddle ye ancient cat's whisker and tune into your favourite programme – if it works, that is."

"That's what we're trying to find out," Venables explained as he plugged in a length of aerial wire to a socket on the back of the case. "OK, we'll try it now! By rights, of course, we ought to rig up the aerial out of doors, but we haven't got time before tea."

He moved away to the far end of the room paying out the aerial behind him, while Atkinson connected his earphones to another socket and twiddled the cat's whisker on the crystal.

There was a hushed silence for a few moments. Then Jennings and Temple called out together: "Can you hear anything?"

Atkinson nodded. "Yes, I can."

"What?"

"I can hear you two bawling, 'Can you hear anything?' at the top of your voices. For goodness' sake shut up and give me a chance to tune my ears in."

The spectators subsided and held their breath as though fearful that the slightest tremor of vibration might upset the delicate precision instrument that Atkinson was now banging with his knuckles in the hope of coaxing some sort of sound out of it.

For a while the radio operator was unsuccessful and then his eyes opened wide in surprise.

"Hey! Wow! Fossilised fish-hooks! I've got a signal coming through," he exclaimed excitedly. "It's going *bleep-bleep . . . bleep-bleep*."

"*Bleep-bleep? . . . Bleep-bleep?*" echoed Darbishire, his eyes blinking in time with his vocal cords.

"Yes. *Bleep – bleep*. Just like that. I must have tuned in to a space-probe rocket!"

"What – on a *crystal set*!" Temple hooted with derision. But the radio operator was only too willing to believe the incredible news.

"Hey, come over here!" he shouted to Venables who was standing on a chair holding the aerial aloft. "I've just picked up a signal from outer space."

Venables grinned as he jumped off his chair. "That was me twanging my penknife on the aerial," he said. "I wondered if it would come through."

After a few more unsuccessful experiments the boys decided that it was a waste of time trying to get results until the aerial was fixed out of doors. They were discussing how and when this could best be achieved when a bright thought skidded over the surface of Jennings' mind.

"Hey, listen! I've got an idea for a great activity for our membership club," he announced. "If we can make this old gadget work with an outdoor aerial we can set up a secret listening post. You know, like the Resistance fighters and blokes like that did, during the war."

The group favoured him with puzzled glances.

"You're bonkers," said Temple. "The *Maquis* and underground fighters like that had to do their listening in secret because it would have been all up with them if they'd been caught."

"So it will be with us if *we* get caught by Old Wilkie," Jennings maintained. "This isn't just a scheme for members to listen to the radio in their free time: it's a top-secret hush-hush listening post."

"Yes, but I don't see the point of . . ."

"Shut up nattering, then," said Jennings, "and I'll tell you all about it."

Chapter 4

Outdoor Aerial

The most exciting feature of Jennings' scheme to set up a secret listening post for the membership club was the fact that discovery would almost certainly spell disaster.

His plan was to rig up the crystal set in different places at different times: in the dormitory, for example, for listening under the bedclothes after lights out; and behind the shoelockers for monitoring important news-bulletins during school hours.

"Supposing there was a Test Match on while we were all cooped up in Old Wilkie's history lesson," he explained to the interested group in the common room. "One of us could leave a book behind in the library and get permish from Sir to go and fetch it. On the way he could pop into the listening post, find out what the score was and pass it round the form when he came back."

"Brilliant!" Temple approved as the possibilities of the scheme grew clearer. "And then, I suppose someone else could find that *he'd* left a book behind a bit later, and pop out for the stop-press results."

"I can't see Old Wilkie standing for that," Atkinson demurred. "By the time they got to the tea interval on the last day there wouldn't be any books *left* in the library at all."

"There's another snag too," Darbishire pointed out. "No Test Matches in February."

Jennings refused to be daunted by such trifling objections. "That was just an example," he said impatiently. Obviously, the first step was to try out the set with an outdoor aerial, and this he planned to do in the dormitory that evening after silence had been called.

"I know we've only got one pair of earphones but that won't matter," he went on. "The guy who's listening can give a running commentary to the others."

"Fat lot of use that'll be," snorted Temple. "There'll probably be a symphony concert going on, and who wants to listen to a commentator saying, 'Somebody's just whamming the big drum'!"

In spite of these criticisms they decided to go ahead with the plan. Accordingly, Jennings and Venables packed up the apparatus and then hurried off to the changing room in the basement to hide the bits and pieces in their shoelockers until bedtime.

As they clattered down the lower flight of stairs they met Bromwich and his friend Rumbelow who stared at the old-fashioned radio with puzzled interest.

"Wow! Whatever have you got there – prehistoric radar?" Bromwich demanded. He snatched the earphones from Jennings' grasp, clamped them on his head and danced about the passage with ludicrous gestures.

"Jodrell Bank calling!" he announced at the top of his voice. "Attention all space-shipping! Here is a gale warning for all satellites north of a line from Mars to Jupiter!"

"Hey, give that back! It's on the secret list and you're not even a member of our club," Jennings protested.

"I *am* a member," Rumbelow maintained. "I've paid my

Jennings seized the earphones and bolted through the open door.

five pence so that gives me the right to know what's going on!"

"Not yet, it doesn't. Not till we've got it all organised."

While the argument was going on Bromwich backed away, intending to make off down the corridor with his booty.

Jennings threw himself forward in a chest-high rugger tackle, seized the earphones from his adversary's head and bolted in through the open door of the changing room. Venables followed with the rest of the equipment and slammed the door shut before Bromwich had a chance to recover.

Gasping from the exertions of the rugger tackle, Jennings locked the door while his companion hid the wireless set in a shoelocker. "We don't want non-members like Bromo showing everyone our secret equipment, or the masters will get to hear about it," he panted.

From the other side of the door Bromwich's penetrating voice could be heard raised in protest.

"Hey, there, you inside! Jennings! . . . Venables! . . . Open the door or there won't half be some bashing-up going on around these parts when we get in."

"Hark at old Bighead!" Jennings shouted back through the keyhole. "We're not letting you in, so crawl back into the woodwork and hibernate."

By now the skirmish was becoming a friendly game with both sides enjoying the exchange of insults. Rumbelow, entering into the spirit of the proceedings, raised his voice above the uproar.

"Death to the traitors!" he shouted in high glee. "They're foreign agents broadcasting with a secret transmitter. Stand by to blow up the building!"

With attackers and defenders bawling at each other

through the panels, the noise in the corridor was considerable. When it was at its height a new sound was added – the thunderous boom of Mr Wilkins demanding to know what was going on.

"Bromwich! Rumbelow! Stop this horrible hullabaloo at once!" The master was obliged to shout with the full force of his lungs to make himself heard as he approached along the corridor. "What in the name of thunder are you boys playing at – yelling through the keyhole like morons screaming at a pop-singer!"

Jennings and Venables exchanged anxious glances. If Mr Wilkins should find out the cause of the commotion their plans for a secret listening post would be discovered. Crouching in silence beside the shoelockers, they listened as Bromwich did his best to assuage the master's wrath.

"We were just – playing a game, sir – that's all!" they heard him explain.

"Game! It sounded more like a revolution."

"Oh no, sir. Just a friendly one, really – with Jennings and Venables. They've locked themselves in and we were pretending they were spies who were hiding from us."

"Locked themselves in, have they! Right! We'll soon put a stop to that nonsense."

There came a rattling of the door-knob followed by a pounding on the panels. "Jennings! Open the door at once, d'you hear?"

Jennings gulped and reached for the key. He was about to obey the order when, on the spur of the moment, he changed his mind, took the key from the keyhole and slipped it into his pocket. Then he scurried across to the window and pushed up the sash.

Outside the basement window was a concrete drainage trench, beyond which a grass bank sloped upwards to the normal ground floor level a few feet above. In a matter of seconds Jennings was through the window and beckoning to his companion to follow.

Venables needed no urging. He, too, had no wish to be confronted by the master on duty at that moment. He scrambled through the window, closed it behind him and followed Jennings up the grass bank on to the playground.

"Famous secret agents escape from enemy fortress," Jennings announced as they reached the top of the bank. "Old Wilkie thinks we're still inside. Let's go and see what's happening, shall we?"

So saying, he led the way round the corner of the building and in through the side door.

As they descended the basement stairs they saw that a crowd of boys had gathered outside the changing room to enjoy the spectacle of Mr Wilkins shouting commands through the jamb of the door – and getting no response!

"Open this door at once!" he was booming in a voice like a loud-hailer. "Stop this silly nonsense, and do as you're told."

Still there was no reply from within and Mr Wilkins' brow creased in a puzzled frown. It was unheard of for his orders to be ignored in this flagrant fashion.

"Perhaps they *can't* open it, sir," suggested Rumbelow. "Perhaps it's got stuck."

"They could answer though, couldn't they!" Martin-Jones pointed out from the depths of the crowd. "Perhaps they've had an accident, sir. Perhaps they both fainted with shock when they heard you blowing your top – er – I mean, when they heard you calling them."

By this time Mr Wilkins was beginning to think that something must be amiss. "It looks as though I'll have to break the door down if I can't get in any other way," he muttered.

Jennings took the key from his pocket and passed it to Blotwell who, with his friend Binns, was hopping about excitedly on the fringe of the group. A nudge, a push and a gesture and Blotwell understood what was required of him. He forced his way through the throng just as Mr Wilkins was preparing to launch the full weight of his fourteen stone at the panels of the door.

"Look, sir! Here's a key, sir!" the messenger squeaked in his penetrating treble. "If it fits, you needn't break the door down – unless you feel you really want to."

Mr Wilkins took the key, inserted it in the lock and found that it *did* fit. He flung open the door and switched on the light . . . Then he turned round to confront Bromwich and Rumbelow hovering anxiously at his heels.

"How dare you play practical jokes on me!" he thundered. "You told me quite definitely that there were two boys locked up inside the changing room, when it's quite obvious that . . ."

His voice tailed away as he happened to glance up and saw the alleged prisoners standing at the back of the group. "Jennings! Venables! What are you doing there?" he demanded.

Jennings' expression was one of wide-eyed innocence.

"*Us*, sir? What are *we* doing here?" he echoed. "We're not doing anything special at the moment; just standing here watching you open the door while we waited for the tea bell, sir."

Mr Wilkins' eye flashed danger signals. The silly little boys had been up to *something* – he was quite sure of that! He suspected that they had been trying to pull his leg, but he wasn't disposed to investigate the matter at the moment – certainly not in the midst of this gawping crowd with asinine grins all over their faces and ridiculous badges all over their sweaters!

He silenced the crowd with a look. "I don't know what's been going on, but it strikes me that some of you boys need your heads examined," he said severely. "And I'm warning you! If anybody else tries on any more funny tricks at my expense – especially *you*, Jennings – I shall – I shall – well, they'd better look out!"

Jennings grinned at his assailants as the tea bell rang and Mr Wilkins strode away up the basement stairs. They'd had a narrow escape: all four of them might well have found themselves in serious trouble . . . But after all, trouble of one sort or another was only to be expected whenever L. P. Wilkins, Esq, was on duty!

For Jennings and his friends in Dormitory Four a far more dangerous hazard still remained – the rigging up of the crystal set and the experiments to follow after lights out.

To begin with, the plan worked smoothly. The apparatus was smuggled up to the dormitory shortly before bedtime, and concealed in a few well-chosen places. The earphones were placed under Venables' pillow, the aerial wire hidden beneath Darbishire's mattress and the small, box-shaped crystal set secreted under a pile of vests and pants in the clothes cupboard.

There was one anxious moment before lights out when Matron insisted on inspecting a dirty mark on Venables' pillow; but somehow discovery was averted, and eventually the master on duty appeared to call silence and put out the light.

41

"OK, the coast's clear. He's gone downstairs," announced Atkinson from his bed by the door, as the adult footsteps died away in the distance. "If we get cracking right away we should be in time for the nine o'clock pop session."

Jennings jumped out of bed, retrieved the radio from the clothes cupboard and placed it on the window-sill. Undaunted by his ignorance of radio engineering, he reckoned that he knew enough to tighten up the loose screws and insert each terminal into its correct socket – even though he was obliged to work by the feeble gleams of a run-down torch battery.

The other boys left their beds and crowded round to help, but in the darkness their efforts caused chaos and valuable time was lost in searching under the beds for nuts, bolts and knobs dropped on to the floor.

After twenty minutes' work Jennings said, "Nearly ready now. Who's got the aerial?"

"I have," replied Darbishire from the darkness on the far side of the bed.

"Righto, then! Chuck it out of the window while I connect up the earth."

"Chuck it out of the window?" Darbishire echoed in surprise. He knew even less about radio engineering than his friend, but all the same this seemed an odd way to treat a vital piece of equipment.

"Well, of course! It's an outdoor aerial, isn't it!"

"Yes, but I thought you wanted to . . ."

"Oh, go *on*, Darbi! Do as I say," Jennings broke in irritably. "We'll never get anywhere if you start arguing about everything."

Darbishire shrugged. "Well, you're in charge of the job, so I *suppose* you know what you're doing," he said doubtfully. Then he lifted the sash and dropped the coil of wire he was holding out into the night.

In the darkness nobody noticed that he had failed to retain hold of one end; and it was some minutes later before Jennings stopped fiddling with the earphones and said, "OK, I'm ready for it now. Pass me the other end, Darbi."

"The other end of *what*?" his friend demanded.

"The aerial, of course. It's a pity we'll have to leave it dangling instead of stretched out, but that can't be helped."

"But I haven't *got* the aerial," Darbishire insisted in aggrieved tones. "You told me to throw it out of the window, so that's what I did . . . It's somewhere down amongst the flowerbeds now."

A moment's horrified silence greeted this shattering announcement.

"You chucked it out of the window?" Venables echoed in amazement. "Crystallised cheesecakes! You must be stark, staring bonkers!"

"Why? That's what you meant, wasn't it? I only did what Jennings told me," Darbishire defended himself. "It sounded a bit funny to me at the time, but he said it was an outdoor aerial so I thought it was all part of the treatment."

Jennings tut-tutted with frustration. "But, you addle-pated clodpoll, Darbi, I meant you to hang on to one end."

"You didn't say so. 'Chuck it out of the window,' you said, so I . . ."

"All right, all right, you needn't tell us a hundred and fifty million times," Temple broke in. "The point is, we're properly up the creek without any aerial. The only thing to do is for someone to go down and fetch it."

In the darkness, the culprit could sense his colleagues' eyes fixed accusingly in his direction.

"Why pick on me? It was Jennings who told me to do it," he protested again. "And anyway you can't expect me to go waltzing out into the garden at this time of night. I might meet someone."

"No, you won't. The masters will be having their supper if you go right away," said Atkinson.

"Yes, but . . ." Darbishire searched his mind for a face-saving excuse. He was appalled at the risks involved. "Anything might happen! Supposing it starts snowing! Supposing I meet an escaped convict!"

"Why should you?"

"I don't know, but supposing I *did* . . . And, anyway, Matron said I wasn't to go out after dark with my cough." A feeble bronchial sound like the yapping of an elderly Pekingese dog broke on the air. "There you are! You can see for yourselves my cough's a lot worse tonight."

"Weedy excuse! You're windy, that's all it is," jeered Temple. "Anyway, you dropped the beastly thing, so it's flipping well up to you to go down and find it."

Fortunately, Jennings rallied to his friend's support. "I'll come with you, if you like, Darbi," he volunteered. "Then one of us can keep watch while the other one looks for it."

Darbishire leaped at the unexpected offer.

"What, honestly? Coo, thanks, Jen." Though still racked with foreboding he felt a little easier in his mind about setting out on his dangerous mission. It wouldn't be nearly so bad if he had a companion, he decided.

He fumbled for his dressing-gown and slippers, and a few moments later the two boys were pattering softly down the stairs to the ground floor.

Chapter 5

Night Operations

No one was about as Jennings and Darbishire crossed the hall. The front door was fitted with a Yale-type lock, so they pushed back the spring latch and clicked it into position to ensure that the door could be opened from the outside upon their return.

Quietly, they let themselves out into the darkness, felt their way down the steps and crept along the playground to the garden beyond. According to their reckoning, the aerial wire should have come to rest in a flowerbed directly beneath the window of Dormitory Four. If all went well it should be the work of a few moments to retrieve the equipment and regain the safety of their room. . . . If all went well! . . .

Half a minute after the front door had closed behind the two boys, Mr Wilkins, having just finished his supper, crossed the hall on his way upstairs to his sitting-room. As master on duty it was his job to make sure that the building was locked up for the night. Accordingly, he glanced at the front door in passing, and his brow creased in a puzzled frown. Surely he had locked that door on his way to the dining hall half an hour earlier! . . . Apparently not, for the latch was fastened back! Odd, he thought. Very odd indeed!

He jabbed his finger at the fitting, the latch flew into place, and Linbury Court was once more secured for the night. Satisfied, the duty master proceeded on his way. . . .

Outside in the garden, Jennings and Darbishire had no trouble in finding the aerial wire and disentangling it from the rose-bush into which it had fallen. Then they scurried back to the main entrance and turned the front door knob.

At once a look of alarm passed over Jennings' face.

"Fossilised fish-hooks, something terrible's happened!" he cried in panic. "The door won't open. We're locked out."

"Perhaps it's only stuck. Push harder," his friend advised.

"I *am* pushing harder, but it's no good. We're caught like rats in a trap."

"Rats in a trap?" Darbishire echoed mechanically, his mind not fully alive to their plight. "But that's crazy. The rats would be trying to get *out*, whereas we're trying to . . ."

"Oh shut up, Darbi! This is urgent. Don't you see, we're properly up a gum-tree now. The catch must have slipped back after we'd shut the door."

"*What!*" Darbishire leaped with shock as the full horror of the situation struck home. "Oh my goodness! This is frantic. We're locked out!"

"Of *course* we're locked out, you great clodpoll! That's what I've been telling you for the last hour and a half, and all you could do was stand there like a spare dinner waffling about rats getting out of traps."

"I'm sorry. I wasn't thinking."

"Well, for goodness' sake start thinking now!"

"Yes, of course." Darbishire tried to think but his brain

was numb with shock. "What are we going to do?" he gulped.

"There's only one thing we *can* do. We'll have to go back and call up to Venables through the window to come down and let us in."

With this in mind they retraced their steps through the garden and began searching for pebbles and gravel with which to attract the attention of the occupants of Dormitory Four.

"How about these?" Darbishire suggested, proffering two stones the size of cooking apples. "It's all I can find in the dark."

"Tut! I said pebbles, not massive great chunks of rock weighing half a ton. If we bung this lot at the window we'll knock Venables and Co. into the middle of next week."

Fortunately, a further search produced a sample of gravel suitable for spattering the window without shattering it.

"Right! Stand by for the moon-shot. Here goes!" Jennings hurled a handful of gravel high into the air.

But not high enough! For instead of reaching the second floor, the stones fell short of their target and rattled a tattoo on the landing window, one storey below.

"Rotten shot. Bad luck!" Darbishire sympathised.

It certainly was! . . . For the unexpected noise reached the ears of Mr Wilkins who had stopped to chat to Matron on the way up to his room. Puzzled, he hurried back along the landing, threw open the window and stared out into the darkness.

"Who's that out there?" he demanded in menacing tones.

The boys crouched in silence in the shadow of the rose-bushes. The question was repeated, then the window slammed shut and the master's silhouette disappeared from the darkened sill.

Darbishire was so frightened that his knees trembled like a blancmange in a railway dining-car. "Oh, my goodness!" he quavered. "Do you think he saw us?"

"No, of course he didn't," Jennings consoled him. "It was much too dark."

"But he knows *someone* must be out here."

"Not nesser-celery – er – necessellarily –" The shock had left Jennings somewhat confused in speech. "He may think it was a very short hailstorm, or a bat hitting against the window."

"A bat wouldn't make that noise – not if it had a rubber handle." Darbishire, too, seemed a little confused, but Jennings let it pass. This was no time for explanations; the need at the moment was to get back indoors as soon as possible.

Jennings scooped up another handful of gravel and took a bearing on the dormitory window. This time his aim was true. The spattering on the pane was followed a few moments later by the window rising and Venables' face peering out into the night.

"That you, Jennings?" he asked in a loud whisper. "What on earth are you still doing down there? You've had time to find twenty aerials by now."

"We're locked out. You'll have to come down and open the front door for us."

"Locked out! You must be bonkers! I should have thought you'd have had enough sense to . . ."

"Ssh! Shut up! This is urgent. I'll tell you about it later."

"Righto!" The head vanished, only to reappear some thirty seconds later with disquieting news. "I can't come down yet. Atki's had a squint through the banisters and

48

he says Old Wilkie's lurking about on the lower landing. You'll have to wait till the coast's clear."

The closing of the window seemed to sever Jennings' and Darbishire's last link with the familiar world of their friends. They were marooned in the middle of a muddy flowerbed on a pitch-black February night, with only their dressing-gowns and pyjamas to protect them from the drizzle of rain which had now begun to fall.

But the chill and discomfort were the least of their worries. What mattered more was whether they had betrayed their presence to Mr Wilkins, and how they were going to get back to their dormitory without being discovered.

"Oh, f-f-fish-hooks, this is f-f-frantic," moaned Darbishire, his teeth chattering like a Geiger counter stuttering over a deposit of uranium. "You are a gruesome ruin, Jennings! It's all your fault."

"Well, I like that," Jennings countered. "Who was the newt-brained shrimp-wit who went and chucked the aerial out of the window?"

"You *told* me to!" Darbishire gibbered in baffled fury. "I wish now I'd never had anything to do with your crazy scheme. I wish I'd never agreed to come downstairs at all. I wish I'd never . . ."

"Oh, shut up," Jennings retorted angrily. "Here we are up to our eyebrows in the most frantic gefuffle since the Peasants' Revolt and you have to stand there making wishes like a fairy godmother in a pantomime. We'll be quite safe if we stay where we are. You heard what Venables said: he'll come down and let us in as soon as Old Wilkie's gone up to his room and . . ."

He broke off as a light flashed on in the staffroom on the ground floor. The curtains were not drawn and from where they stood the boys could clearly see into the room.

The sight chilled their rapidly congealing spirits to rock-bottom zero. . . . Far from going upstairs to his sitting-room like a civilised human being, Mr Wilkins was making preparations to search the grounds in his zeal to solve the mystery of the noise at the window. Reasonable explanations such as sudden hailstorms or low-flying bats just didn't seem to have occurred to him at all.

Transfixed with dismay, Jennings and Darbishire watched as the master pulled on his raincoat and (obviously expecting violence) took a hockey stick from the cupboard to use as a weapon.

The staffroom light switched off. Seconds later the front door opened and then shut with a loud click as Mr Wilkins set forth into the school grounds on the track of any intruder, trespasser or burglar who might be lurking outside in the darkness.

The sight of his form master marching down the front steps brandishing a hockey stick set Darbishire's overstrained nerves twanging like guitar strings.

"Oh, my goodness! Whatever are we going to do?" he gasped in a terrified squeak.

"Run!" Jennings answered firmly. "Quick, before he gets us in focus!" He turned and scuttled back along the grass path between the flowerbeds, but he had not gone five metres before he realised that his companion was not following.

"Come on, Darbi – *run*!" he urged in a tense whisper.

"I can't run. My bedroom slippers keep dropping off."

"Carry them, then. Run in your bare feet!" Jennings went back and seized his friend by the arm, and propelled

Mr Wilkins set forth into the school grounds.

him barefooted and hopping into a nearby shrubbery where they crouched in the shelter of a laurel bush.

They could not see Mr Wilkins, but away to their left they could hear him poking through the undergrowth in search of the unknown intruder.

"He's bound to find us. He's making his way towards us," Darbishire quavered.

"All right, don't panic! We'll wait till he's behind that clump of bushes by the Head's garden, and then make a dash to somewhere safer."

Behind the sports pavilion on the far side of the football pitch would be a good place to make for, Jennings decided. It was, of course, impossible to predict Mr Wilkins' movements, but the chances were that having scoured the immediate vicinity without result he would abandon his search. And by that time, with any luck, Venables would have had a chance to slip down to the front hall and unlock the door.

"Get ready to follow me," Jennings whispered. "And for goodness' sake try not to make a sound."

He put out a hand to steady his friend's shaking shoulders. If only old Darbi could stop his teeth rattling like castanets, they'd stand a better chance, he thought.

Darbishire swallowed hard and prepared to follow his leader. The prospect of playing hide-and-seek with Mr Wilkins round the rose-bushes on a cold, wet night was not one that appealed to him. "This is the last time I'm going to get roped in for any of your crack-brained schemes," he said miserably. "Definitely the last time."

Meanwhile, upstairs in Dormitory Four, Venables, Temple and Atkinson had been discussing how best they could help their colleagues marooned in the garden. They were unaware that Mr Wilkins, without a thought for his own safety, was patrolling the grounds like a faithful watchdog to protect them from any malefactors – real or imaginary – who might be lurking within the precincts.

"He's bound to have pushed off to his room by now," Temple said when five minutes had ticked away. "Nip out on to the landing, Atki, and see if the coast's clear."

Atkinson's report was reassuring: there was no sign of life in the hall. So after arguing for some minutes as to who should undertake the rescue operation, Venables got out of bed and crept down the stairs.

The front door was locked as Jennings had reported. Venables pushed back the latch and fixed it in place, then opened the door and looked out.

He had expected his colleagues to be hovering close at hand and was surprised that he could see no sign of them. He wandered out on to the top step. Then in the distance he heard someone moving about amongst the flowerbeds. What on earth were old Jen and Darbi playing at, he wondered?

He strained his eyes in the direction of the sound, and was about to call to his friends by name when the moon came out from behind a cloud and silhouetted a large adult figure poking the roots of a syringa bush with a hockey stick as though looking for a lost ball.

Venables recognised the adult figure. Had Mr Wilkins taken leave of his senses, he wondered? Civilised people, however keen they might be on outdoor games, didn't play hockey up and down the flowerbeds all by themselves on a cold, wet, February night. Football by floodlight – yes! Hockey by moonlight – no!

Then the significance of the master's actions struck him. It certainly wasn't a *hockey ball* that he was looking for!

Hurriedly, Venables slipped back into the hall. It

wouldn't do for Mr Wilkins to know that yet another member of Dormitory Four was out of bed and downstairs after lights out. Venables shut the door, leaving it unlocked as he had agreed, and then sped upstairs to report the latest development to Temple and Atkinson.

"Wow! Poor old Jen and Darbi," Temple sympathised when he heard the news. "I wouldn't like to be in their shoes when Old Wilkie gets them in his gunsights. What d'you think we ought to do about it?"

"There's nothing more we *can* do. I've unlocked the door so it's up to them now." Venables hopped back into bed and sat upright with his ears cocked for sounds of activity in the garden below.

Chapter 6

The Key to the Mystery

By the time Mr Wilkins had made his way round the garden and poked through the shrubbery without finding any trace of an intruder, he decided to abandon his man-hunt. Perhaps he had been mistaken, he thought. Perhaps it *had* been a gust of wind that had rattled the landing window!

He turned and strode back towards the building, unaware that the objects of his search were crouching in the bushes behind the sports pavilion on the far side of the football pitch.

With his hockey stick tucked under his arm he mounted the steps and took his latchkey from his pocket. He was about to insert it in the lock when, by chance, it slipped through his fingers, hit the top step with a slight *clink* and slid away in an unknown direction. Muttering at his carelessness, he stooped and groped about in the darkness, but without a torch to aid him the search was useless.

If only he had left the door on the latch instead of slamming it behind him, he reflected. Now, he would have to ring the bell and cool his heels on the doorstep until somebody happened to hear him – whenever that might be! For at this late hour the domestic staff had gone off duty and the masters had dispersed to their rooms.

That was one of the annoying aspects of boarding school life, he reminded himself: at certain times of the day an unexpected visitor could stand ringing the front door bell for hours on end and nobody would even *hear* – let alone answer the summons.

After five minutes of frustrated bell-pushing, Mr Wilkins relieved his feelings by impatiently rattling the door handle. . . . To his surprise the door swung open and, caught off balance, he stumbled forward, tripped over the sill and only stopped himself from falling flat on his face by performing a complicated hopscotch dance halfway across the hall.

When he had recovered he went back and examined the lock with a puzzled expression on his face. He was quite sure he had fastened the door behind him when he went out. He had heard the latch click into place, and as a precaution he had given the door a final push to make certain it was secure. Why then had it swung open at a touch on the handle?

It was most mysterious – especially as this was the second time that evening that he had found the door unfastened. Perhaps the lock was faulty!

At the moment, however, he was more concerned about finding his latchkey than speculating on the eccentric behaviour of spring door-locks. Mr Carter had a powerful torch which would be just the thing for a search of this kind, he remembered. He would go and borrow it without delay.

Mr Wilkins shut the front door and made sure that it was properly fastened. Then he went upstairs to his colleague's study on the first floor.

"I say, Carter, I wonder 'f you'd lend me your torch," he began as he strode into the room with his usual heavy-footed tread.

"Yes, of course." Mr Carter looked up from the pile of exercise books before him and noticed the weapon which his visitor was still holding. "Bit dark for hockey practice, isn't it?" he inquired drily. "Even with the aid of a torch."

Mr Wilkins looked a little sheepish. "I thought I heard someone outside in the garden, so I went to have a look," he explained. "Then I dropped my key on the step and I couldn't get in. I was ringing for at least five minutes, but nobody answered the bell."

"And how *did* you get in?"

"Well, actually, the door wasn't locked after all."

Mr Carter frowned at his colleague as though harbouring doubts about his sanity. "But you just implied that it *was*. You said you couldn't get in."

Mr Wilkins rubbed his nose with the crook of his hockey stick and the puzzled expression came back into his eyes. "That's the mysterious thing about it," he confessed. "I know it was locked when I went out, and it was definitely open when I came back. And it was playing the same sort of trick just after staff supper!" He narrowed his eyes with renewed suspicion. "Perhaps there *is* something funny going on! Perhaps I *did* hear somebody outside, after all!"

Mr Carter refused to be stampeded into believing that anyone was lurking in the school grounds with criminal intent. "Let's not worry about burglars. Let's go and look for your key," he said, rising to his feet and reaching for his torch.

It was five minutes after Mr Wilkins had finished prowling round the grounds before Jennings decided it was safe to leave their hiding place.

"He can't *still* be stonking around, or we'd have heard him," he told Darbishire as they crept out from behind the pavilion. "Put your bedroom slippers on and follow me, and for goodness' sake don't make a row."

The drizzle had stopped, but the wind was chill as they approached the school building. Jennings, who was a few paces in the lead, was the first to reach the door. As he turned the handle he stiffened and caught his breath in dismay.

"Hey, Darbi, the door's still locked!" he whispered.

"No, it isn't; it *can't* be. Venables said he was coming down to open it."

"Well, *you* try, then!"

Darbishire came hurrying up the steps and seized the knob, unable to believe that still another blow could be added to their misfortunes.

"What a frantic bish!" he moaned when the door refused to yield. "Venables has doublecrossed us, that's what's happened. The rotten, treacherous traitor! Just wait till I see him again! Just wait till I get my hands on him! Do you know what I shall do? I shall . . ."

"Yes, well, never mind that now," Jennings broke in. Interesting though the topic might have been on some other occasion, this was hardly the moment, he felt, to listen to Darbishire's detailed description of the tortures he proposed to inflict upon Venables at some unspecified time in the future. "Besides, it may not be his fault. Old Wilkie came back this way, don't forget. He probably locked the door after him."

"Old Wilkie! Yes, of course! Oh my goodness! What on earth shall we do, then?"

Jennings pulled a long face. "There's only one thing we *can* do. We'll have to go and get hold of Venables and . . ."

"Oh *no*! Not *again*! Not all that ghastly throwing-gravel-at-the-windows caper all over again!" Darbishire danced with exasperation, and the movement sent one of his ill-fitting bedroom slippers flying into space. "Oh fish-hooks, now look what's happened!" he wailed.

"How can I look? It's too dark to see anything," Jennings retorted irritably. "I can hardly see my hand in front of my face."

"Never mind your hand! Or your face either. It's my *foot* I'm on about. I've lost my slipper."

Jennings had little sympathy to spare for troubles as trifling as this. He hurried off down the steps muttering, "Well, you look for it, then, while I go and get Venables."

As he reached the bottom of the steps there was a loud cry of anguish from his friend at the top. Shocked, he turned and called urgently into the darkness, "*Ssh!* Darbi! For goodness' sake, *ssh!* Someone will hear you."

"I couldn't help it. I'm hurt. I trod on something sharp with my bare foot," Darbishire whispered back. He stooped and removed the offending object from between his toes. "It's a key."

"What!" Jennings turned and pounded back up the steps with renewed hope. "Perhaps it'll open the door!"

Darbishire snorted and said, "Huh! You've got a hope!"

For by now he was so stricken with woe that he couldn't believe that a stroke of good luck would ever come his way again. *Other* people, locked out and benighted, who happened to stub their toes on latchkeys might well find that they had stumbled upon the very thing they needed to turn disaster into success . . . But that wouldn't happen to *him* – Charles Edwin Jeremy Darbishire! Oh no! In his case the discovery was more likely to be yet another trick played on him by an unkind Fate.

"I shouldn't be surprised if this rotten old key opens every rotten old door in the whole school *except* this rotten old one," he said, bitterly.

"We can soon find out, can't we!"

Jennings took the key from his friend's fingers and fumbled in the darkness to find the lock. "Keep your fingers crossed while I see if it fits. If it does, we'll be laughing!"

As the two masters descended the stairs, Mr Wilkins continued to ponder the events of the evening in his mind.

"I still don't understand it," he persisted in puzzled tones. "That noise I heard on the window: finding the door unlocked, like that. It *could* have been burglars, you know."

"I doubt it," replied Mr Carter. "What you heard was probably Matron's cat knocking over a flowerpot or something."

"Nonsense!" Mr Wilkins retorted as they reached the hall. "I tell you I distinctly heard a—"

He broke off and stiffened. "*Ssh!* There's somebody outside! I heard voices."

The two men strained their ears to catch the sound. Sure enough, a faint low-pitched muttering could be heard beyond the closed front door.

"There you are! I was right," Mr Wilkins breathed excitedly. He brandished his hockey stick like a life-preserver. "Come on, let's go and—"

"Stay where you are," Mr Carter advised. He had heard a faint metallic scraping at the keyhole. "I think they're coming in."

In two seconds Mr Wilkins was across the hall, crouching beside the door as tense as a panther poised for the kill.

Again there came the metallic scraping as the key fumbled round the lock and then slid into place. . . . The catch eased back, the handle turned and the door moved a few cautious inches.

As it opened wider Mr Wilkins flexed his muscles for the pounce – and then drew back in baffled amazement. . . . For into the hall crept a furtive procession of two.

In the lead was J. C. T. Jennings bearing a coil of aerial wire, followed by C. E. J. Darbishire wearing one bedroom slipper and holding up his trailing dressing-gown like a crinolined dancer performing a minuet.

"*Doh!*" Mr Wilkins shot up like a fighter-pilot on an ejector-seat. "What – what – what on earth's going on here?"

Both boys leapt with shock. They had not expected to find anyone waiting in the hall.

"Oh, sir, you gave me a fright, sir," Jennings gasped. "I thought you'd – er – I thought you would have gone up to your room by now."

"Why should you think that?" Mr Carter demanded from across the hall.

Jennings hesitated. It was impossible to pass off the situation with a few airy words of explanation. He would have to confess.

"Well sir, we – sort of – happened to be behind the pavilion when Mr Wilkins was – er – going for a walk, sir."

Mr Carter took the news calmly. "H'm! That certainly accounts for the so-called burglars – and the unlocked door," he observed. "I'm glad we've found the key to the mystery at last."

"Oh no, sir! *This* isn't the key to the mystery. *This* is

the key to the front door," Jennings explained, holding out the object for the master's inspection.

Mr Wilkins was rumbling like a thunderstorm deciding where to break.

"Yes, yes, yes, but what in the name of reason were you silly little boys doing outside in the first place?" he demanded, raising his hockey stick aloft like a banner in a protest demonstration. "I've never met such fantastic behaviour in my life! Running round the rose-beds in pyjamas and dressing-gowns an hour after lights out. What's the meaning of this appalling conduct?"

Jennings fidgeted with the coil of wire he was holding. "It was this, sir. Darbishire dropped it out of the window by accident, so we had to go and get it."

Mr Wilkins eyed the tatty length of wire with suspicion. "What is it?" he barked.

"Our aerial, sir. You see, we were going to try out an old radio set in the dorm – just to improve our education, as you might say, by listening to symphony concerts and – er – educational lectures and things."

"What!" A strangled squawk of indignation forced its way through Mr Wilkins' vocal cords. He waved his arms in the air and stamped his feet as though practising a dance-step without music.

"Disgraceful!" he boomed. "Radios under the bed-clothes! You ought to be ashamed of yourselves – especially you, Jennings! You'll bring the set to me first thing in the morning and – and –" He searched his mind for a suitable punishment. "And you'll stay in and work instead of playing football every afternoon from now until half term."

"Yes, sir."

Low in spirit, the culprits plodded upstairs to bed where

in hushed tones they recounted the tale of their misadventures to the other occupants of the dormitory.

Venables was incensed at the news that his crystal set was to be confiscated.

"It's not fair! It wasn't even my fault," he protested. "You are a crazy clodpoll, Jennings! I wish now I'd never had anything to do with your mouldy old listening post."

Jennings felt a twinge of remorse on Venables' behalf. "I'm sorry about your old radio set, honestly," he apologised as he sat up in bed, trying to think of some suitable compensation. "How would it be if we made you a Vice-chairman of the membership club to make up for it?"

To his surprise the offer was accepted. "Yes, all right then," Venables agreed. "It's quite a fair swap really, because we'd never have been able to hear anything on that old radio, even if Darbi hadn't bunged the aerial away."

"What makes you so sure? We'd got it all fixed up," said Temple.

"Yes, I know, but it still wouldn't have worked. You see, I dropped it in the changing room when Jennings and I were hiding from Bromo, and I'm pretty sure I busted the cat's whisker."

There was silence for a few moments while the significance of this remark sank in. Then a long gasp of outraged indignation sounded from Jennings' bed by the window.

"Well, I like that! Of all the gruesome swizzling chisellers!" he burst out. "You land poor old Darbi and me in for the most frantic hoo-hah of the twentieth century, and now you calmly turn round and tell us it was all for nothing."

"Oh, I wouldn't say that. I wouldn't say it was all for

nothing," Venables replied, taking a broadminded view of the events of the evening. "You see, even if the set *didn't* work I knew we'd all get quite a lot of fun out of trying to fix it up – especially *you*, Jennings!"

Chapter 7

Contact

The untimely collapse of the plans to set up a secret listening post did nothing to restore the reputation of the Jennings Membership Club as an institution capable of organising worthwhile activities.

Indeed, for some days after the fiasco, Jennings felt too depressed to do anything about it. Darbishire did his best to keep the ball rolling by rounding up members for the exchange of matchbox labels; but this, it was felt, was a poor showing for a club whose organisers boasted of arming its members with stratosphere space-guns complete with deafening sound-effects.

The stockpile of badges and free tokens continued to grow, though by now Jennings and Darbishire had to rely on Mrs Hackett to collect the material on their behalf. This was because their services in the dining hall had been dispensed with when Miss Matthews, the housekeeper, found them having chariot races with the dinner trolleys up and down the room.

The term was approaching its halfway mark and Matron, after some weeks of coping with outbreaks of minor ailments, was hoping to clear the sick-room of invalids before the weekend break.

On the Wednesday before half term the only occupant

was Bromwich, who had arrived after football the previous afternoon. He was up and dressed, and scheduled for release later in the day, but he seemed in no hurry to go.

"Don't you think it'd be better if I went back into school tomorrow, Matron, instead of today?" he suggested as she tidied the sick-room in preparation for the doctor's visit.

"I certainly don't. You're bursting with health and vigour," she told him. "I'd have sent you back after breakfast only I wanted the doctor to have a look at that ankle."

"It's still swollen, Matron. People like old Martin-Jones shouldn't be allowed on football pitches if they can't tell the ball from somebody's ankle, should they? I was just going to shoot and he came zooming along and . . ."

"Yes, I know. You've told me four times."

Bromwich sighed. If he could delay his return into school for twenty-four hours he would miss Mr Wilkins' weekly French test. He lowered his injured foot to the floor with suitable grimaces of pain and hobbled across to the window.

"When I walk with a limp, like this, you'd think I'd got a wooden leg, wouldn't you?" he asked hopefully.

"I doubt it. The way you were running round the room when I came in just now I thought you were training for a four-minute mile."

The patient ignored the implied rebuke. "If I'd *really* got a wooden leg I could keep my socks up with drawing-pins, couldn't I!" he pointed out.

Matron raised despairing eyes to the ceiling and went out of the room. She had a great deal to do: with so many boys going out at the weekend there were clothes to be checked and a multitude of tasks awaiting her attention.

Five minutes after her departure, as Bromwich was practising his wooden-legged limp round the table, a light footstep sounded in the corridor and Jennings poked his head round the door.

"Hullo, Bromo! How are you getting on?" he began chattily as he advanced into the room. "Lucky old you! You'll miss Old Wilkie's French test if you . . ."

"Stop! Get out! You can't come in," Bromwich protested urgently. "Matron will go into orbit if she finds you in here."

Jennings hesitated. The sick-room was strictly out of bounds to everyone except the patients. The rule was rigidly enforced in the interests of the boys' health, and anyone entering the room without permission was liable to find himself in very serious trouble.

"It's all right; it's quite safe. She's downstairs nattering to Mr Carter and Old Wilkie," the visitor explained, as though this fact would keep him immune from any germs that might be floating about in the atmosphere. "Darbi told me you'd decided to join the club after all, so I just popped in to bring you your membership badge."

"You needn't have bothered."

"Well, I thought if you were stuck in here, not feeling well, it'd cheer you up a bit. You could sit and look at it when you'd got nothing to read."

The Chairman advanced to the table and pinned the little plastic disc on to the new member's sweater.

"There you are! I hereby invest you with all the rights and privileges of the Jennings Membership Club."

"Thanks. How's the club going?" Bromwich wanted to know.

"Famously! We're doing all sorts of fantastic things."

"Such as what?"

The Chairman considered. "Well, we *were* going to have this secret radio station, only Darbishire bished it up, so we're back to matchbox tops for the moment. But you just wait till the space-guns come," he went on hurriedly before the new member could start criticising. "*Wheee-ooomph! Wheee –*"

The whine of the missile stopped abruptly as Matron's voice was heard in the corridor, calling to Blotwell to tuck his shirt in.

"*Emergency red!* You've had it this time and don't say I didn't warn you." Bromwich spoke in the satisfied tones of one who himself has nothing to fear. "Allow her five seconds for chivvying-up Blotwell, and she'll be in here dropping the next pay-load right where you're standing."

Escape was out of the question, with Matron so close to the door. The only thing to do was to take cover.

Of the eight beds in the sick-room, only one looked like providing a possible hiding place. This was the bed in the far corner, set against the wall. Jennings dived underneath it and lay flat on his face while Bromwich pulled the bedcover nearly down to the floor to screen him on the side exposed to view. Then he draped a towel over the foot-rail, and was just completing the work of camouflage when Matron came into the room.

The next few minutes were fraught with uncertainty. Matron busied herself about the room getting things ready for the doctor's visit. She didn't actually look underneath the beds, though there was an anxious moment when she dropped a towel so close to where the fugitive was lying that he might well have been discovered had she stooped to pick it up. With great presence of mind, Bromwich skipped across the room and retrieved it for her. He showed a surprising turn of speed for one suffering from such pain that he couldn't face Mr Wilkins' French test.

Matron showed no sign of leaving and Jennings began to

grow desperate. He was doubtful whether he could remain in his present uncomfortable position much longer without revealing his presence. To make matters worse the floor had been polished that morning by Mrs Hackett who, in her usual slap-happy way, had upset a tin of strong-smelling floor-polish under the bed where he was hiding. Then, after five minutes which seemed like five hours, he heard the sound of a car drawing up on the playground below.

Bromwich heard it too. He glanced out of the window and said, "Here's the doctor, Matron. Hadn't you better go down and let him in?"

"He knows the way," she replied, and Jennings' hopes fell, only to rise again when she went on, "Perhaps I'd better have your health record-card handy in case he wants to see it."

She hurried out to fetch it from her filing cabinet in the dispensary, and Jennings crawled from his hiding place and leaped to his feet.

"Quick! Now's your chance! She'll be back in two shakes of a cow's tail," said Bromwich.

Jennings needed no urging. He skidded through the door and shot off down the landing like a rat down a drainpipe.

The incident had left him badly shaken. He liked Matron too much to derive any pleasure from deceiving her. He'd have to be careful, he told himself severely. This was no way to behave towards someone who very nearly headed his list of Top Ten favourite people for the first half of the Easter term.

Venables was alone in the common room when Jennings, still breathless from his escape, panted in through the door.

"There's a parcel for you," Venables greeted the new-comer. "You weren't here when Mr Carter dished them out, so you'll have to wait till he comes down again. It was only a small one, so it couldn't have been the space-guns."

"I know. We haven't sent up for them yet. We were waiting till we'd got enough – er . . ." Just in time Jennings remembered that the source of supply was a secret. "We shall probably write and order them tomorrow."

Venables nodded. "Well, if there's anything to eat in your parcel, remember that I was the first one to tell you about it. Don't think I'm hinting, but if it hadn't been for me you wouldn't have known about it until . . ."

He broke off, frowned, and sniffed hard. "What's all that muck you've got down the front of your sweater?"

"Oh, that's nothing. Only floor polish," Jennings explained, smearing the stains over a larger area. "I went up to the sick-room to take old Bromo his badge. I thought it'd be company for him."

Venables glanced at him with sudden suspicion. "You didn't go *in*, did you? You didn't actually go *near* him?"

"Yes, of course I did. I pinned it on for him. And then I heard Matron coming so . . ."

"You must be bonkers. You won't be allowed out at half term if she gets to hear about it."

"Not allowed out? Why ever not?"

"Because you've gone and put yourself in quarantine, that's why," Venables replied in tones of fascinated horror. "If you've been in contact with Bromwich and he's suffering from, say, for instance, bubonic plague or the Black Death or something, you'll have to be isolated."

That aspect of the encounter hadn't occurred to Jennings; after all, Bromwich had *looked* healthy enough.

He listened with growing concern as Venables recalled tragic examples of boys who, in the past, had violated the privacy of the sick-room and had paid dearly for their folly.

There was the case of Martin-Jones who, the previous Easter term, had smuggled a box of Turkish Delight to a measles-stricken friend, and had himself come out in a rash that same afternoon. As it happened, the rash was traced to irritation from a scratchy woollen vest, but it had been a nasty shock all the same.

Then there was Rumbelow, caught red-handed distributing comics to convalescents in the final phase of a summer epidemic of mumps. Although he hadn't contracted the complaint himself, his action had involved the whole school in a further period of quarantine, so that all cricket matches had had to be cancelled for the rest of the term. As Venables pointed out, this had done nothing to increase Rumbelow's popularity with his friends.

Finally, there was the awful warning of Blotwell who, owing to a similar act of bravado, came out in spots on the very last day of the winter term and had to spend Christmas in bed at school when everyone else had gone home for the holidays.

Jennings' face was grave and the wide-awake look died out of his eyes as he listened to the grim recital.

"Yes, but all these blokes got caught. Matron didn't see me so there's nothing to worry about, is there!" he pleaded in defence.

"There certainly is! It's not *you* I'm worried about – it's *us*," Venables retorted, backing away to a safe distance. "If you've picked up some of old Bromo's germs we may all come out in spots before Saturday, and then *we* shan't be allowed out with our parents either."

At that moment Temple came into the room and advanced upon the suspected germ-carrier with a friendly smile. "I say, Jennings, there's a parcel for you," he began. "If it's anything to eat you won't forget that I . . ."

"Stand back! Stand back!" Venables cried dramatically. "Keep away from Jennings whatever you do."

Temple wheeled round in surprise. "Why, what's the matter?"

"He's got chicken-pox."

"I *haven't* got chicken-pox," the suspect denied indignantly.

"Well, mumps, then – or whooping cough or whatever it is old Bromo has got."

"Old Bromo?" echoed Temple.

"Yes, he's ill. He went up to the sick-room yesterday after football."

"I know that," Temple replied. "But it wouldn't be whooping cough, because he had it last term. Probably measles, this time."

Venables held his handkerchief to his face to avoid breathing the contaminated air. "There you are then, Jennings. That proves it. You've got measles!"

Temple narrowed his eyes and peered closely, but was unable to detect any signs. "Are you *sure*, Ven?"

"You just said so yourself, didn't you! If Bromo's got measles, then Jennings must have too, because he actually touched him."

"But he hasn't got any spots."

"Ah, not yet, but you just wait. He'll probably come out in a terrific scarlet rash on Saturday morning, just as his aunt comes prancing up the drive to take him out."

A number of boys had drifted into the common room

as the medical discussion was going on. Venables thought it only right to warn them of the danger in their midst.

"Mind out, Atkinson! Stay where you are! And you too, Rumbelow! Everybody keep away from Jennings if you want to go out on Saturday. He's got mumps."

"I haven't! I haven't!" shouted the accused. "And anyway, you said it was measles just now, so that proves you don't know what you're talking about."

"What does it matter which one? They're both infectious."

There was a general movement towards the other end of the room.

Rumbelow produced a small telescope and trained it on the suspect from a distance of fifteen feet. "I can't actually see any mumps-bumps at this range," he reported in a voice tinged with disappointment.

"I shouldn't go any nearer, though. Nobody knows how far these germs can jump," Temple advised.

The precautions taken to avoid the risk of infection resulted in a certain amount of confusion when Mr Wilkins arrived a few minutes later to compile the usual list of boys in need of a haircut. He was accompanied by Mr Carter carrying some letters and a parcel, and both masters were surprised to find such a dense concentration of boys huddled together at one end of the room. At the other end, a lone and silent figure was staring mournfully out of the window.

"Right! Come along now, you boys. All get in a straight line!" Mr Wilkins commanded as he strode in ahead of his colleague. "I want to see which of you needs a haircut. No one is going out with his parents on Saturday with the back of his neck looking like the coastline of Norway."

There was a shuffling, but no real movement from the

tightly packed group. No one seemed anxious to start the queue.

"Quickly, now! I haven't got all day to waste," Mr Wilkins urged. He began chivvying the boys into some semblance of order and noticed that the lone figure by the window was making no attempt to co-operate. "Wake up, Jennings! Come and stand here between Johnson and Nuttall."

As Jennings took his place in the middle of the queue, the boys on either side slipped away and joined on to the far ends of the line. This was repeated by the boys next to them who now found themselves in the contaminated area and hurried to get out of it as quickly as they could. In a matter of moments, Jennings was again standing all by himself while two disorderly queues jostled for places at opposite ends of the room.

Mr Wilkins eyed the antics of the queue-jumpers with amazement.

"Venables, Temple, Atkinson! Where on earth d'you think you're off to? Come back here and line up properly," he boomed.

"Can't we line up over here, sir? There's – er – there's more room," Temple pleaded.

"*More room!*" This was preposterous! They were squashed together like apples in a cider press.

"Well, perhaps not actually more *room*," Temple conceded, as the pressure of the crowd sent him lurching into a bookcase. "But we shan't waste so much space if we all stay over here."

The two masters exchanged puzzled glances.

"They've all gone off their heads," Mr Wilkins said with a shrug of resignation. "There's no other way to explain it."

"I'm afraid it's me, sir," said the lone figure in the middle of the room. "Nobody wants to stand next to me."

"Why not?" Mr Carter asked.

"Well – er – because they think they won't be able to go out with their parents on Saturday."

"Why should they think that?"

Jennings shuffled his feet and said nothing.

"He's in quarantine, sir," said a voice from the crowd. "He's got chicken-pox. He's got to be insulated."

"Oh, sir, I *haven't* got chicken-pox," Jennings protested.

"Well, measles, then."

Mr Carter's brow creased in a frown of bewilderment. "I don't understand, Jennings. Are you feeling ill?"

"Oh no, sir. I'm feeling fine. It's just that . . ." He paused wondering how to explain his lapse. "Well, perhaps I was rather rash but . . ."

"Rash! There you are! I knew it was measles," Temple informed Atkinson in a whisper of ghoulish satisfaction.

". . . but unfortunately I went into the sick-room to see Bromwich without permission, and everybody says I'm in quarantine for – er – whatever it is that Bromwich has got, sir."

Mr Wilkins bridled indignantly. "In the sick-room without permission! Scandalous! Never heard of such a thing!" He glanced at the unhappy culprit fidgeting from foot to foot in shame and mortification. "Very well then, Jennings! You've brought this punishment on your own head. You'll have to go back to the sick-room and stay there."

"Oh, but sir, that's not fair. I don't want to be insulated – er – isolated," Jennings protested. "My aunt's coming down specially on Saturday to take me out and . . ."

"You should have thought of that earlier, before you started breaking school rules," Mr Wilkins retorted brusquely. "Go upstairs and find Matron. Tell her you've been in contact with Bromwich, and that you're a suspected case of – of . . ."

He broke off as the door swung open and Bromwich, looking the picture of health, strolled into the room.

Chapter 8

Wholesale Distribution

The boys in the common room stared at the newcomer as though he were some visitor from a world beyond their own. Mr Wilkins, too, seemed taken aback by the unexpected turn of events.

"I – I –! What are you doing here, Bromwich?" he demanded. "Why aren't you in bed in the sick-room?"

"In bed, sir?" Bromwich echoed in surprise. "Oh, I didn't have to stay in bed, sir – it wasn't as bad as all that. And now the doctor's been, Matron said I could come back into school. I'm quite all right again now."

Mr Carter smiled and said, "We're all delighted to hear it – especially Jennings! It was believed in well-informed circles that you were suffering from – er – let me see – what was it?"

"Measles, sir," prompted Temple.

"Chicken-pox," suggested Atkinson.

"No, it wasn't; it was mumps," said Martin-Jones. "Either that or whooping cough."

"Precisely," said Mr Carter. "Purely as a matter of interest, Bromwich, what exactly *was* your complaint?"

"Oh, I didn't *complain*, sir. I rather enjoyed being in the sick-room."

"You misunderstand me," Mr Carter explained. "I

meant what was the illness that you were suffering from?"

"Oh, I see! A rather nasty bruise on my left ankle, sir."

"Eh! Well of all the . . ." Mr Wilkins smote his brow in a gesture of despair. "Tut! Silly little boys! All that ridiculous fuss about nothing!"

"Yes, sir. Martin-Jones accidentally kicked me during football and Matron kept me upstairs because she wanted the doctor to have a look at it, but he said it was all right." Bromwich demonstrated his fitness by performing an improvised hornpipe and marking time at the double. He couldn't think why everyone was so interested in the details of his trivial indisposition, but he felt rather flattered by their attention all the same.

Jennings had more reason than anyone else to rejoice over Bromwich's return to health. He turned to Mr Carter and asked, "Does that mean I haven't got to be insulated after all, sir?"

Mr Carter nodded. "Yes, Jennings. Neither insulated nor isolated. According to the best medical opinion, there is no period of quarantine laid down for being in contact with a rather nasty bruise on the left ankle."

"Phew! Thank goodness for that!" Jennings sighed with relief. He'd be able to go out with Aunt Angela after all!

"Mind you, there's still the matter of your going into the sick-room without permission to be considered," Mr Carter went on. "You'd better come and see me in the staffroom after tea and we'll – ah – have a little talk about it."

"Yes, sir!"

After that, the line-up for hair inspection proceeded smoothly; and when it was known that Jennings had a parcel awaiting him, he was overwhelmed by offers from boys inviting him to stand next to them in the queue.

"I'm reserving a special place for you next to me," said Atkinson who, two minutes earlier, wouldn't have touched him with a barge pole.

"No, come over here, Jennings! It's quieter by the window," urged Martin-Jones.

When the inspection was over, Jennings collected his parcel from Mr Carter. It was from Aunt Angela – he could tell that by the writing – and he was mildly surprised that she should have sent him a gift so soon before her visit.

However, there was no point in wasting time speculating on Aunt Angela's motives when hungry friends were breathing down the back of his neck urging him to cut the string and see what lay inside. He would rather have been left to open his parcel in peace; but there was no chance of that, for now his company was being sought as eagerly as it had been shunned a few minutes before.

The parcel, when opened, was found to contain a box of chocolates of moderate size. Jennings offered one to Darbishire and then passed the box round amongst his friends.

"Hey, watch it, Jen! You won't have any left for yourself," Darbishire cautioned as the top layer vanished before his eyes. "You must be crazy opening it in here with everybody swarming around like vultures with their tongues hanging out. Why didn't you keep it till afterwards?"

Jennings shrugged. "Too late now. Besides, I'm feeling in one of my generous moods, now I haven't got chicken-pox, after all."

Even so, the donor was inclined to regret his generosity shortly afterwards when the crowd drifted away champing their jaws and licking their lips. There were only two chocolates left in the box. "Might as well finish them up," he said, tossing one to Darbishire and popping the last one into his mouth.

He threw the box into the wastepaper basket and was crumpling the parcel's brown paper wrapping when he noticed a sheet of writing-paper half concealed amongst its folds. Muttering in self-reproach, he picked it up. Stupid of him to have overlooked Aunt Angela's letter! It was probably to tell him what time she was arriving on Saturday. He straightened out the crumpled sheet and read aloud:

"Dear John,
     Thank you for your letter. I was sorry to hear that you had been in bed with a sore throat last month and am glad that you are now up and about again. It will be nice to see you at half-term. Would you like to bring one of your friends out to lunch with you? . . ."

He broke off and grinned at Darbishire. "Hear that! You can come too if you like."

"Coo, thanks!" Darbishire was only too pleased to accept the invitation, for his own parents were unable to pay him a visit. "Really generous of your aunt, taking us both out *and* sending you a box of chocolates as well."

"Yes, she is generous, isn't she," Jennings agreed. "Unless you happen to rub her up the wrong way; and then she can be a bit awkward. However . . .!" He returned to the letter:

"I hope you remembered to thank Matron for looking after you while you were in bed. I expect you were disappointed at not being able to give her a box of chocolates as you had intended, so I am sending . . ."

His voice faltered and he stared at the letter in dismay.

"Oh, *no*!" groaned Darbishire. "Don't bother to read any more. I can see what's coming!"

"So can I," Jennings replied grimly. He ran his eye down the page. "You're dead right! She says I'm to give the chocolates to Matron as a present from me for all the trouble she went to, making my sore throat better."

He screwed up the letter, shook his head and sighed deeply. "Tut! Women!" he muttered in tones of quiet despair. "Women! Aunts, Matrons – the lot! You never know what they're going to do next, do you!"

Darbishire was too shattered by the latest development to protest at the injustice of this remark.

"So those chocs weren't yours after all," he said reproachfully. "Never intended for you at all, and now you've gone and eaten the whole box."

"*I* haven't eaten the whole box. Other people have."

"Same thing. They were Matron's chocolates all the time. They weren't meant for you in the first place, and now look what you've done."

Jennings banged his fist on the table in exasperation. "All right, all right, all right," he squawked angrily. "You don't have to tell me a hundred and fifty million times they weren't meant for me. If you'd said so *before* I'd given them away, there might have been some sense in it."

He was annoyed with himself for being so impulsive. If he'd thought of it earlier, he would have been only too delighted to give the chocolates to Matron, whether they had been intended for her or not.

"Well, it's too late to do anything now. She'll just have to go without," Darbishire remarked. "After all, if you don't tell her, she won't know what she's missing, so she can't very well blow her top about it, can she?"

But this easy solution failed to take account of the fact that Aunt Angela would be visiting the school on Saturday and would certainly exchange a few words with Matron, if only to thank her in person for nursing her nephew back to his usual state of robust health. She would expect Matron to make some reference to the gift, Jennings pointed out; she might even broach the topic herself.

"I bet you a million pounds, the first thing Aunt Angela will say is: 'Well, Matron, how did you like the chocs John gave you?' or, 'Did you like the hard ones better than the soft centres?' or something like that," Jennings maintained, as he outlined the shape of snags to come. "And then it'll all come out about my eating them myself and handing them round wholesale. She'll never believe it was an accident! I know Aunt Angela!"

Darbishire pursed his lips as he realised the gravity of the situation. It seemed to him that even if the excuse of the unfortunate accident was accepted, it was hardly the sort of thing that would put Jennings' aunt in the most generous frame of mind when the time came to order lunch at a Dunhambury hotel. "What a ghastly shemozzle!" he lamented. "It's enough to make your mind boggle."

"I know! Mine's boggling on both cylinders," Jennings confessed. A thought struck him and he added, "I wonder if we could get any of them back before it's too late! Atkinson said he was going to keep that second one I gave him until after he'd had his hair cut."

"Yes, and there was the one with a nut on top that

Binns took for Blotwell because he was doing his music practice."

But a moment's reflection convinced them that the prospect of salvaging any of the chocolates was too fantastic for serious consideration. Their only chance lay in explaining the situation to the boys who had taken part in the share-out in the hope that some of them would be able to replace the chocolates they had eaten with contributions from some other source.

The tea bell rang. Jennings retrieved the box from the wastepaper basket and with his handkerchief wiped it clean of the old stamp hinges, apple-peel and pencil sharpenings that were sticking to it.

"Well, at any rate, we've still got the box," he said hopefully. "All we've got to do now is to find some chocolates to put in it. Matron will be as chuffed as two coots when I give them to her. She'll never know they aren't the proper ones."

He looked up to see Darbishire staring into space and stroking an imaginary beard – a gesture which he claimed always helped him to think more clearly.

"What's up with you, Darbi! Had a brainstorm?"

"Not exactly, but I've just had an idea of where I might – I only say *might* – be able to lay my hands on a few chocs to put in the box."

"Goodo! Where?"

"A few chocs to put in the box," Darbishire repeated. The phrase seemed to give him a great deal of pleasure. "How's that for a home-made poem on the spur of the moment! *Chocs* rhyming with *box*! I bet old Wordsworth couldn't have done it as quickly as that!"

"Never mind the poetry: where are you going to get them from?"

"I can't tell you that. It's a sort of secret supply that I know of; something to do with my . . ." No, better not to mention the cough mixture, he thought. Too risky! "It's a secret supply that I happen to know of."

"You can tell *me*, can't you?" Jennings urged.

"Well, I'd rather not, because then it wouldn't be secret any more." Darbishire was firm on this point. "Besides, it may not come off; it doesn't always work, but if it *does*, it'll be peppermint creams."

Jennings decided not to probe more deeply. "Fair enough," he agreed. "The sooner you find out if it's working the better. Peppermint creams will be all right. I don't suppose we'll be able to get all the same kind anyway, but if we can fill up with a mixed assortment it'll be better than nothing."

"Yes, of course. Can't afford to be fussy in a crisis," Darbishire agreed as he made ready to go downstairs to the dining hall. "After all, it's the thought behind the gift that really matters, isn't it!"

The response was not encouraging when, during tea that evening, Jennings appealed to the boys at Form Three table for contributions towards the mixed assortment. It was not that his colleagues were unwilling, but rather that in the last few days before half term no one had any sweets – or, indeed, tuck of any description – left in his tuck-box. Had the appeal come a week later there would have been a different story to tell.

"I could owe you some sweets and let you have them after my parents have been," Venables suggested when he realised Jennings' dilemma. "They always stock me up with a massive supply to last till the end of the term."

"That's too late. It's got to be *before* my aunt and

Matron get together and start swapping notes," Jennings explained. He frowned thoughtfully and mashed his baked beans into an unappetising pulp. "Surely there must be a few blokes in the school who have still got some tuck left, if only we knew who to ask!"

Temple had a bright suggestion. "Why not let the membership club organise a scavenging hunt?" he said. "If everybody has a go, we're bound to rake up something between us."

His neighbours looked at him with increased respect. It wasn't often that old Temple had any worthwhile ideas to put forward.

"Yes, why not! It'll be a change from Darbi's mouldy old matchbox tops while we're waiting for the space-guns," Atkinson observed. "We could call it the ordinary members' good turn to the Chairman for generously giving us all free guns – when they come, that is."

After some discussion it was planned to pass the word round that a club meeting would be held in the common room the following morning after breakfast. The main item on the agenda would be the collection of offerings to fill the chocolate box to be presented to Matron when it was ready.

"And what's more, I shall also be making an announcement about the space-guns," said Jennings importantly. The stock of tokens kindly collected by Mrs Hackett had been mounting daily and by the end of the week he reckoned he would have enough to send away for the long-awaited weapons.

"Goodo! I was beginning to think we'd have to whistle for them," said Martin-Jones. "The trouble with most of old Jennings' famous wheezes is that they come unstuck at the seams before they really get going!"

Jennings gave him a knowing smile. "Not this one! I've got it all worked out," he said confidently. "Just you start tracking down a few chocs for Matron's tuck-box and leave the ballistic missiles to me."

Chapter 9

Costly Mistake

Jennings awoke on Thursday morning eager to get to grips with the problems of the day.

He had a full programme before him. First, an appointment with Mrs Hackett to collect the tokens she had been saving for him ever since his domestic duties had been so abruptly curtailed. Then there was the club meeting to receive donations towards Matron's tuck parcel. After that, he and Darbishire would get down to the important task of writing to the manufacturers of Krunchie-Whispie cereals for the consignment of space-guns to which their free tokens entitled them. They'd have to enclose a letter with the tokens, he decided, explaining the reason for such an unusually large order.

"I don't suppose many of their customers could save up a hundred and fifty-odd coupons as quickly as we have," he confided to Darbishire as they hurried downstairs together as soon as they were dressed. "That's where we're lucky, having everybody in the school, including masters, eating Krunchie-Whispies specially for us, as you might say. But you just think of an ordinary small family trying to collect all that lot in about a fortnight. They'd have a terrible time!"

He pursed his lips in sympathy as he pictured the scene

in his mind's eye: the neat suburban house with mother, father and two children seated, bloated and gasping, round the dining table for hours at a time, forcing down huge platefuls of their never-ending diet of cornflakes; the dog's dinner bowl and the cat's drinking saucer piled high with cereals; the budgerigar's song silenced by the carbo-hydrates crammed into its crop; a blanket of soggy flakes coating the surface of the goldfish tank!

"Come along now! Don't give up hope!" the father was encouraging his overfed offspring, as he reached for yet another packet. "Only another half-hundredweight of valuable vitamins, and we'll have enough missiles to equip the whole neighbourhood."

The indigestible vision faded as Jennings led the way to the dining-hall door. Mrs Hackett, still wearing her plastic passport to the space age pinned on her overall, was setting out cups and saucers at the masters' table.

"She's been ever so good to us, cutting out the coupons for us and all that," said Jennings. "I reckon we ought to give her a little present."

"Box of chocs?" suggested Darbishire.

Jennings gave him a look. "Don't be funny!" he said.

Mrs Hackett glanced up and advanced to meet them with a cornflake carton stuffed with the tokens she had been collecting on their behalf.

"There you are then – and that's your lot," she told them thrusting the container into Jennings' hand. "Won't be no more where those came from. We're going over to a different sort for a week or two, Miss Matthews says."

"That's all right. We've got enough now," Jennings assured her. "And thanks awfully for keeping them for us. We couldn't possibly have managed without you." Surely there must be *some* way in which they could show their appreciation! He thought for a moment and went on, "We're having a meeting of our club after breakfast. Would you like us to put your name forward as an Honorary Vice-President?"

Mrs Hackett looked doubtful. "What's that going to land me in for?" she demanded suspiciously.

"Oh, it wouldn't cost you anything – not even the annual subscription."

"Five pence per person per annum, or per part of per annum," the Treasurer quoted from the rules. "It'd be an honorary honour you see, so in a way we'd be saving you five pence a year."

"I don't think I'll bother," she decided. "I wouldn't want to go running around with one of these space-guns you're always on about. Nasty, dangerous things, I'd say."

"You don't *have* to have a gun – it's not compulsory," the Chairman assured her. "Still, if you don't want to be a Vice-President we won't nag you about it."

With the cornflake packet concealed under his sweater, Jennings led the way downstairs to the basement. They had decided to use the boiler room for the task of counting the tokens and making up the parcel, for only here could they rely upon finding the privacy needed for carrying out a secret operation of this kind.

As expected, the boiler room was deserted. Robinson, the odd-job man, had already stoked up the fires for the morning and was unlikely to return for some while.

Darbishire switched on the light and shut the door, as his companion perched himself on a pile of coke and produced the packet from under his sweater.

"We'd better keep an eye on the time. You can't hear the breakfast bell down here," Jennings said, wriggling to make himself comfortable on his knobbly seat. He tipped the cardboard discs on to the floor. "Now, let's see what we've got here!"

They counted the tokens and stacked them in neat piles. There were a hundred and fifty-six – three more than they needed to accompany their order.

"That's all right, then." Jennings started shovelling them back into the packet. They were both in high spirits at the thought that from now on the project would be all plain sailing. "And we'd better think what we're going to say in the letter, hadn't we!"

"You bet!" Darbishire waggled his head in glee and said: "Dear Mr Krunchie-Whispie, I hope you are quite well." He cackled with laughter at the absurdity of the phrase. "Can't very well call him that, can we! Or how about: 'Give my love to Mrs Krunchie-Whispie and all the little cornflakes.'"

Carried away by the brilliance of his so-called wit Darbishire collapsed, helpless with mirth, on a heap of coke. There was no responsive laughter from his companion, so he went on, "Didn't you hear what I said! I said, 'Give my love to . . .'"

He broke off and glanced at his friend in surprise. Far from appreciating the joke, Jennings was staring at the cornflake packet in his hand as though it were a time-bomb about to explode.

"What on earth's the matter with you, Jen? You look as though you've just seen the ghost of Hamlet's father."

It was some moments before Jennings could bring himself to reply. Then, in a strained, unnatural voice he said, "We've had our chips this time, Darbi. We've gone and cooked our goose properly. Made a complete hash of it."

"Hash? Goose and chips?" Why this talk about food all of a sudden? Darbishire wondered.

"We've made the most gruesome bish in history. Those space-guns *aren't* free – they cost two pounds each, as *well* as the tokens; it says so on the packet."

"*What!*" Darbishire shot from his coke heap like a startled rabbit; his mouth gaped and his eyes goggled. "But they *must* be free! You told me so yourself."

Jennings passed him the carton. "It's all Miss Matthews' fault," he said bitterly. "Ever since she stopped us doing the breakfast we haven't even *seen* a cornflake packet close to, let alone had a chance to read it. We'd have found this out ages ago if it hadn't been for her."

Darbishire read the details in small print. Then he cleaned his glasses on the hem of his sweater and read them again, as though hoping that the film of coke-dust on the lenses had caused him to mis-read the instructions. . . . But there was no doubt about it: anyone anxious to take advantage of the Special Offer had to include a postal order with his application.

Darbishire put the packet down with trembling fingers. His face had the expression of a springboard diver who, having leapt high into the air, realises too late that the swimming-bath has been drained of water. "Oh, my goodness," he moaned. "Whatever are we going to do!"

Jennings flapped his fingers in despair. He could have kicked himself for so carelessly jumping to the wrong conclusion. And now that a meeting of the membership club had been arranged for after breakfast the situation was desperate. They would all be expecting him to announce when the promised weapons would arrive. All the fine promises he had made! And all the confident boasting – and now this!

"What on earth am I going to tell them?" he demanded. "They'll tear me limb from limb: they'll wipe the floor with me if I stand up and say there won't be any guns after all."

Darbishire nodded. "A lot of the blokes only joined because of the free gift," he pointed out. "They'll think the whole thing's an organised swindle to diddle them out of their five pences."

"I know! We'll have as much chance as two mice at a cats' tea party when they start chucking the furniture about."

"*We!*" The Hon. Secretary gulped slightly and crossed his fingers. As an official of the club he realised that he, too, could expect to share in the rough treatment when the members turned truculent.

"I suppose there's no one who'd lend us the money?" he said, without much conviction. "Your Aunt Angela, for instance, or someone like that."

Jennings snorted. "Are you fooling! She wouldn't lend me the lolly for *one* space-gun, let alone fifty!"

"But you said she was generous."

"Ah yes, but she doesn't approve of people having guns. She's keen on disarmament."

Darbishire felt that he and Aunt Angela saw eye to eye on this matter. *He* didn't approve of people having guns either – well, not at a cost of two pounds each which somebody else had to pay.

"Perhaps we could start our own disarmament campaign," he said hopefully. "If we could persuade blokes that they didn't really *need* these space-guns, they might agree to cancel their orders."

Across the room a chink of red light shone through the jamb of the damper on the furnace. Jennings walked over to it, opened the fire-box door and tossed the carton with its hundred-and-fifty-six tokens into the flames.

Then he turned back to Darbishire and said, "You wouldn't have a hope! If Aunt Angela can't make politicians and generals and people see that they don't really need all these weapons, what chance have you and me got against pig-headed clodpolls like Venables and Co.!"

They discussed the matter at some length, but they knew there was nothing they could do to stave off the disaster awaiting them at the hands of the irate members of the club.

Jennings sighed. The wide-awake look went out of his eyes and his shoulders slumped in dejection.

Darbishire had nothing further to say, and for some while they stood brooding in silence, quite unaware that the breakfast bell had sounded twenty minutes earlier and that the rest of the school had long since finished their Krunchie-Whispies and were halfway through their bacon and fried bread.

At about the same time that Jennings and Darbishire were hurrying off to the boiler room to count their tokens, Rumbelow came downstairs from his dormitory to find a parcel awaiting him in the front hall.

Parcels were exciting objects, especially when they were unexpected, and Rumbelow succumbed to temptation. By rights, he should have waited until the post was given out by the duty master; but as the postman had only just left the front door it was safe to assume that no one in official circles knew of the parcel's existence – and never *would* know if the owner spirited it away before the duty master appeared on the scene.

He picked up the package and made off to the bicycle shed on the far side of the playground to open his parcel in private. On the way he met Bromwich who insisted on accompanying him and being present at the opening ceremony.

"You can come if you like, but it's nothing to eat, honestly," Rumbelow told him.

Bromwich sounded shocked that his friend should harbour unworthy suspicions. "I never thought it *was* anything to eat," he said with injured pride. He ran his fingers over the parcel and squeezed it. "It *could* be food though, couldn't it!" he added hopefully.

"No, it couldn't. It's from my grown-up sister. She's not interested in food; she says we get too much as it is."

In the bicycle shed Rumbelow produced a penknife and hacked off the wrapping. Inside was a cardboard box with a highly-coloured label depicting a youthful marksman peppering a distant target with deadly accuracy. Along a dotted line indicating the path of the marksman's aim the word *WHEEE-OOOMPH!* was blazed out in jagged, eye-catching capitals.

The Stratosphere Spring-loaded Ground-to-Air Space-Gun read the caption beneath the picture. *Complete with Battery-operated Resonator and One Dozen Missiles.*

"Wow! What a beauty!" Rumbelow breathed as he opened the box and held up the weapon for his friend's approval. "It says on the lid that it shoots sixty feet. Let's go and try it out. We've just got time before the bell goes."

Outside on the playground Martin-Jones, Venables and other third-formers, having a few minutes to spare before breakfast, were engaged in an improvised game of hockey with a dented ping-pong ball and school rulers. They abandoned the game and came crowding round to inspect Rumbelow's new possession at close quarters.

Everyone agreed that the weapon was a first-class piece

of equipment. When examined (unloaded) the resonator vibrated with ear-splitting volume and the spring trigger seemed fully strong enough to justify the manufacturers' claims of a sixty-foot trajectory.

When the chorus of admiration had died down, Venables said, "I don't get this! Surely this is the same gun that Jennings is going to hand out free to all the membership club. It's exactly like the one he told us about."

"That's right. Identical," Martin-Jones agreed. "Lucky old Rumbelow! He'll have *two* when old Jennings starts dishing out the free ones."

"Yes, but what about the expense?" Venables persisted. "I don't know how much they cost, but three or four dozen of this little old gadget would put paid to anyone's pocket money for about ten years!"

Venables' statement produced puzzled frowns and solemn nods of agreement. Where on earth was old Jennings getting the money from? Had he come into a fortune?

"Well, he's given his promise now, so he can't get out of it," said Martin-Jones. "Pretty generous of him, anyway."

"He's always pretty generous. Look how he handed round Matron's chocolates," Venables pointed out. "I vote we pass a vote of thanks to him at this meeting after breakfast. That'll show that we trust him not to let us down."

"Supposing he does – what then?" queried Bromwich.

Venables narrowed his eyes and stuck out his jaw in a pugnacious attitude. "Just let him *try*, that's all," he said with spine-chilling menace. "Just let him *try!*"

All this time, Rumbelow had been examining his space-gun and arming it with its payload of plastic missiles. Now he was ready for action.

"Stand back, everybody," he cried. "Ye famous sixty-foot demonstration is now about to take place!"

The point at which they were standing appeared at first glance to be an ideal site for testing stratosphere space-guns. To the right was an open space leading away to the football pitches and the grounds beyond. Behind them and to their left was the main school buildings consisting, at ground level, of the dining hall, kitchen, staffroom and classrooms, and terminating with the headmaster's study at the extreme end of the L-shaped block. Straight ahead a wide gravel drive swept down to the main gates.

Rumbelow was anxious not to lose any of his ammunition by firing into the open country of the football field where recovery of the little plastic marbles might prove difficult. If he was careful to fire straight ahead, the missiles were bound to land on the drive. Here they could be easily seen and retrieved without any trouble.

He forced back the spring, loaded the weapon and squinted along the gunsight. . . . As his finger was squeezing the trigger, Bromwich suddenly squawked, "Hey, careful, Rumbo! The Head's watching you out of the study window! . . ."

Chapter 10

The Mixed Assortment

M. W. B. Pemberton-Oakes, Esq, M.A. (Oxon), was a headmaster who, as a rule, was content to leave much of the day-to-day routine of the school in the capable hands of Mr Carter and his colleagues. For this reason he seldom attended school breakfast in the dining hall and usually made his first appearance of the day at morning assembly.

On Thursday, however, he decided to vary his routine. Shortly before eight o'clock he entered his study and stood admiring the view of the copse beyond the football pitches while he waited for the breakfast bell to ring.

He noticed a small cluster of boys chatting together on the playground and displaying an interest in some toy (he could not identify it at that distance without his glasses) which one of their number appeared to be showing the others.

Mr Pemberton-Oakes smiled indulgently. He was a kind-hearted man with progressive ideas, and he liked to see the boys out in the fresh air before breakfast occupying themselves with interesting and harmless pursuits.

He moved closer to the window and stood watching. . . .

"Hey, careful, Rumbo! The Head's watching you out of the study window!"

It was unfortunate that Bromwich chose to bark out

his warning at the very second that the marksman was preparing to let fly.

Startled, Rumbelow jerked his head in the direction of the study window; the gun swerved in his hand and the trigger, adjusted to a hair's breadth, tightened under his grasp and discharged the weapon with the full force of its spring-loaded mechanism.

Wildly off course, the plastic projectile whistled away to an unscheduled target as, automatically, the battery-operated resonator enclosed in the gunstock screamed out its bloodcurdling sound-effect . . .

WHEEE-OOOMPH!!!

It was all over in a split second. The study window shattered into a thousand fragments and Mr Pemberton-Oakes leaped for cover behind his rolltop desk.

When the fragments had ceased falling, he emerged cautiously and stood upright. He was not hurt – the missile had cleared him by a foot and come to rest in the fireplace – but he was badly shaken and very angry indeed . . . Few headmasters, however progressive they may be, feel at their ease when shot at by trigger-happy third-formers at so early an hour in the morning.

He went back to the window and looked out. Some twenty yards away was a group of boys frozen by shock into motionless statues like a "still" photograph from a film of violent action. They stood rooted to the spot, their eyes glazed with horror, their mouths agape with dismay, unable to believe that this terrible thing had really happened . . . Few third-formers, however headstrong they may be, have much taste for attacking headmasters with ground-to-air missiles before breakfast.

There was no need for Mr Pemberton-Oakes to open the window. He put his head through the glassless frame

Mr Pemberton-Oakes leapt for cover

and called out, "Come here, the boy who did that!"

Rumbelow detached himself from the stupefied group. He walked towards the house like one in a trance, his stratosphere spring-loaded space-gun, complete with battery-operated resonator, hanging limply from his trigger finger.

From inside the building a bell shrilled out its cheerful morning summons. It was time for breakfast.

Nobody ever knew what passed between Rumbelow and Mr Pemberton-Oakes in the headmaster's study. So far as the school was concerned the outcome was a speech, short and to the point, which the headmaster delivered when he arrived in the dining hall halfway through the meal. He marched straight up to the masters' table, called for silence and held up Rumbelow's ill-fated space-gun so that everyone could see it.

"Do any more of you boys own one of these murderous contraptions?" he demanded, twirling the weapon in his fingers as skilfully as a sharpshooter in a Wild West television serial.

Nobody did!

"Right! Now listen to me, everybody; listen carefully because I've got something important to say."

Seventy-seven of the seventy-nine boys of Linbury Court School laid down their knives and pricked up their ears. The remaining two boys (listed on the register as Darbishire, C. E. J., and Jennings, J. C. T.) heard nothing of the headmaster's proclamation for they were still downstairs in the boiler room, ignorant of the shattering events of the previous twenty minutes.

"These dangerous gadgets are absolutely forbidden in this school," Mr Pemberton-Oakes announced. "No boy is to write away to order one, or buy one from a shop – so remember that, when you go out with your parents on Saturday."

He was so intent upon pressing home the point of his lecture that he failed to notice the two vacant places at Form Three table. He continued: "Furthermore, if anybody is sent one of these horrible things in a parcel from home, or receives one from any other source, he is to hand it over immediately to one of the masters. Is that clearly understood?"

The boys nodded and went on with the bacon and fried bread which they had been holding uneaten between their jaws while the headmaster was speaking; while at the top table Mr Pemberton-Oakes sat down to a belated breakfast of coffee and Krunchie-Whispies, quite unaware that there was any connection (*via* Rumbelow's grown-up sister) between the appetising cereals on his plate and the alarming experience which he had recently undergone.

Downstairs in the boiler room, Jennings looked at his watch. "Fossilised fish-hooks, it's twenty-five past eight!" he exclaimed in dismay.

Darbishire looked up in alarm. "Oh, my goodness! They'll all be out of breakfast in two bats of an eyelid!"

Time had stood still for the Chairman and Hon. Secretary of the membership club. Aghast at the wreck of their plans, they had spent the best part of twenty minutes in futile discussion of what they could do to fulfil their obligations.

Jennings jumped to his feet and hurried out of the boiler room with Darbishire at his heels. They were not worried at having missed their breakfast, for neither of them had any appetite for the meal. All the same, they had some qualms (unnecessary as it happened), in case their absence had been noted by some member of the staff.

The boarders were coming out of the dining hall as the two boys reached the ground floor. Venables spotted them and called out, "All set for the meeting? I'm just going down to my tuck box to get my contribution. See you in the common room!"

Jennings gave him a wan smile and turned to his companion. "Come on," he said. "Let's go and face the music."

"Wait a minute!" said Darbishire, forcing his mind away from the subject of space-guns. "Those peppermint creams I told you about. I'll go and see what I can do." He made off up the stairs towards the dispensary.

There was already a fair sprinkling of members present when Jennings reached the common room, and by the time Darbishire had got back from his secret journey nearly a couple of dozen had assembled for the meeting.

Tense with foreboding, the Chairman rose to deliver his address. His throat was dry and butterflies fluttered in his stomach.

"Well, as you know, the main thing about this meeting is so that we can get together a mixed assortment for Matron," he began awkwardly, dreading the thought of what he would have to say next. "Only before that, I've got an unfortunate thing to tell you. I'm terribly sorry, but I shan't be able to let you have those space-guns I told you about, after all."

He stopped and braced himself for the expected storm of protest, while Darbishire standing beside him measured the distance to the door with his eye, weighing up their chances of a quick getaway before the fur began to fly.

But no storm broke; no fur flew. Instead, the members

nodded in sympathy and waited for the Chairman to continue.

Jennings was taken aback. Hadn't they understood? Hadn't he made himself clear? "So that means there won't be any free space-guns after all," he repeated nervously. Still there was no reaction from the members who, by rights, should now be setting about the unfortunate officials like a wolf-pack descending on a sheep-fold.

Jennings was flabbergasted. "Don't you – don't you *mind*, then?" he asked in puzzled wonder.

"Well, of course we *mind*. We're just as disappointed as you are," Venables replied on behalf of the audience. "It's just one of those things. We've got to put up with it."

"That's right," added Atkinson. "We're not blaming *you*, Jen. We know it's not *your* fault."

The Chairman and Hon. Secretary exchanged bewildered glances. What was the matter with everybody that they should accept this unforgivable breach of faith without a word of protest? For days past they had been pestering the club officials for a firm delivery date and threatening reprisals if they were let down. And now this! It didn't make sense! Had the shock of the announcement unhinged their minds?

"Well, it's very good of you to take it like this," Jennings said meekly. "It just shows what a friendly lot of blokes we've got in this club, doesn't it!"

In point of fact, it showed nothing of the sort, but it was not until later in the day that he and Darbishire heard about the headmaster's ban and realised how Rumbelow's misfortune, rather than the good nature of their fellows, had saved them from a very awkward predicament.

Having disposed of the space-guns, the meeting got

down to the main item on the agenda. Jennings produced the chocolate box and said, "I hope everybody's been able to rake up some decent things for Matron. We can't have any spaces, or she'll think I've been having a little nibble on the quiet."

Several of the members had been inspired by Temple's suggestion at tea the previous evening to go round the school collecting remnants of tuck from any source they could find. Now, they came trooping forward and laid their offerings upon the common-room table.

It was not an impressive sight. Martin-Jones, Bromwich and Nuttall, working as a team, had gathered together one toffee, two boiled sweets, an extremely sticky date and three cubes of jelly.

Jennings jabbed a disdainful finger at the last-mentioned item. "Is this the best you could do? I can't give Matron these."

"It's all right; they're not cooked," Martin-Jones assured him. "We got them from Mrs Hackett when she was doing the masters' supper."

Darbishire's contribution was more orthodox – four peppermint creams. "From my private source," he said mysteriously.

Temple was carrying his pencil box as he pushed his way through to the front. "Couldn't find much, I'm afraid. Hardly anybody's got any tuck left," he apologised. "Still, I haven't come empty-handed." He tipped up the pencil box and two acid drops and a piece of sugar-coated chewing-gum fell on to the table.

"Good job it's not for Old Wilkie! He can't stand chewing-gum," said Martin-Jones. "He nearly went into orbit when he found me with a piece in my handkerchief during prep the other night."

Jennings was eyeing the collection in dismay. "But I can't put hunks of raw jelly and bits of chewing-gum in," he protested. "It's meant to be a presentation box of chocolates."

"Assorted sweets, Jen," Darbishire corrected. "Call it that and you can put in pretty well anything."

"Yes but . . ." Jennings turned to the next donor. "What have you got, Venables?"

"Three lumps of sugar."

"*What?*"

"Well, they're sweet, aren't they? Lots of people like sugar lumps. Horses love them."

"Matron isn't a horse, you clodpoll."

"Put them on the bottom layer, then, and she won't see them to start with," Venables advised. "And I've got these, as well!" He fumbled in his pocket and produced two liquorice allsorts, stuck together, that he had found at the bottom of his tuck box.

"Sorry they're a funny shape," he apologised. "They were underneath my roller skates. Should taste all right, though."

Jennings flipped his fingers in exasperation. "This is hopeless," he complained. "I was expecting some *proper* contributions." He glanced up at Atkinson who had just arrived at the table. "I only hope to goodness you've found something a bit better than this other lot."

Atkinson considered. "Well, actually, I couldn't actually get hold of any actual sweets, as you might say," he explained. "But I've found something just as good – better, actually."

With a flourish he whipped a packet of cough lozenges from his trouser pocket and added it to the growing pile on the table.

"They're genuine best quality, sugar-coated cough sweets," he proclaimed as though selling his wares in the market place. "Everybody likes them. Of course, it's even better if you've got a sore throat as well, but you don't actually *have* to have a . . ."

"All right. Thanks very much," Jennings interrupted somewhat curtly. "I'm terribly grateful to all you lot – don't think I'm not; but honestly . . ."

He sighed and ran his eye over the contributions – the chewing-gum, the sugar lumps, the throat pastilles, the sticky date. . . . It was all very well to talk about a mixed assortment, but apart from Darbishire's peppermint creams, this was too much of a mixture to suit *anyone's* taste. He couldn't give Matron a present that looked as though it had been salvaged from the sink-tidy!

Hopping about amongst their elders were Binns and Blotwell, the youngest boys in the school. Their presence was barely tolerated by those of riper years but, as members, they insisted on remaining as a gesture of the rights of the rising generation.

They squeezed their way through to the front and peered at the unappetising confectionery on the table. Blotwell wrinkled his nose and said, "Looks a bit of a mess, doesn't it!"

"Shut up, Blotwell, nobody asked you," said Martin-Jones, shocked at this lack of respect from one so young.

"Well, I was only going to say . . ."

"Don't say it; we're not interested."

Blotwell shrugged. "All right then, I won't." He turned to his companion. "Come on then, Binns, let's go. They don't want to hear how we could make this old garbage look like a box of sweets on a telly advert."

106

He made for the door, but Jennings called him back. "How?" he demanded.

"Camouflage," said Blotwell. "Binns and I have been collecting sweet wrappers and silver paper off chocolates and things ever since the beginning of the term. We were having a competition to see who could get the most."

"We've brought them with us," added Binns, producing a small toffee tin from under his sweater. "Thought they might come in useful, as we hadn't any actual sweets to give you."

He turned the tin upside down and a cascade of sweet-wrappings of the best quality floated down on to the table. Gold, silver, multi-coloured; transparent and opaque; deckle-edged foil and striped cellophane – an artistic, eye-catching collection worthy of the most expensive sweets and chocolates that anyone could wish for.

"All smoothed out ready to use again," he said. "Form One's contribution to Matron's tuck box, with compliments from Blotters and me."

Jennings flashed him a grateful smile. "Coo, thanks! They'll be just the job." He picked up one of the jelly cubes and wrapped it in a square of tasteful crimson paper backed with silver that had at one time housed an exotic chocolate truffle. "How about that! At least they'll *look* all right, whatever they taste like."

Darbishire had his doubts. "That's all very well, but what happens when they're unwrapped?" he argued. "That'll give the game away, won't it!"

Murmurs of assent arose from the group. "That's right! You'll be properly up the creek when that happens," they agreed.

The youngest boy in the school turned to his elders and gave them a short lecture in adult psychology.

"You needn't bother about that," Binns said with all the confidence of his eight years and six months. "Grown-ups aren't choosey about sweets in the way we are. So long as it's got a classy-looking bit of paper round it, they pop it in without looking and don't seem to notice the taste."

"And if they do," added Blotwell, giving them the benefit of his more mature experience (he was three weeks older than his friend), "if they *do* notice it, they don't like to say anything because it's not polite, so you're bound to be all right either way."

Chapter 11

Gift Horse in the Mouth

The bell was ringing for morning assembly when the meeting closed and the members dispersed. There was no time then to do anything but scoop the contributions and the wrapping papers into the chocolate box and leave the arrangement of the contents until later.

Jennings was hoping to do this at break, but Mr Carter insisted on everybody being out-of-doors in the late February sunshine. An attempt after the midday meal was frustrated by the duty master holding a shoe inspection, and it was not until the free hour before bedtime that Jennings had a chance of getting down to his task.

When it was finished, everyone agreed that the camouflage was a work of art. Without removing the wrapping there was no way of telling – well, *hardly* any way – that what might have been a delicious walnut-topped, strawberry-flavoured, soft-centred chocolate was actually a flattened liquorice allsort surmounted by a sugar lump.

"How about that! Not bad, eh!" the craftsman exclaimed as his colleagues clustered round to admire his handiwork. "I'll give it to her on Saturday when she has us up for the old spit-and-polish parade."

There was no school on the Saturday morning of half-term weekend. Instead, boys who were going out had to report to the dispensary so that Matron could make sure that visiting parents were not greeted by offspring with missing shirt buttons, broken shoe laces or grimy finger-nails.

A carefree, light-hearted atmosphere always prevailed on these occasions. With school rules relaxed and thoughts of work banished until Monday, Matron's inspection was an enjoyable prelude to the excitement of going out for the day, and meeting mothers and fathers again after six weeks' absence.

When Jennings and Darbishire, looking unbelievably clean and tidy, reached the dispensary at half past ten, about a dozen boys were grouped about the room telling one another at the tops of their voices what they were hoping to persuade their parents to let them order for lunch. Mr Carter and Mr Wilkins were also present, checking the arrangements of the boys who were going out.

Matron gave the newcomers a brief inspection. "Tuck your shirt in properly, Darbishire. My goodness, you certainly had a close hair-cut last Thursday! You're both going out with Jennings' aunt, I understand."

"That's right, Matron," said Jennings. He produced a package wrapped in clean tissue paper salvaged from a laundry basket, and thrust it into her hands. "My aunt asked me to give you this box of choc – er – I mean, this mixed assortment – for looking after me while I was in bed with my sore throat."

Matron took the parcel and unwrapped it. "That's very kind of her – very kind of you both. Thank you very much."

Any hope that she would refrain from opening the box until the donor was safely off the premises was shattered when she removed the lid and said, "They look lovely! I think it would be rather nice to hand them round, don't you?"

"Well – er –" But before Jennings could think of any delaying tactics, she had offered the box to the two masters, both of whom accepted with smiles of thanks. After that she passed the mixed assortment round so that all the boys present could help themselves.

Most of them had taken some part in the preparation of the gift two days before and so were able to indulge in a fascinating guessing game as they made their choice – which of the tastefully camouflaged sweets were, for example, the peppermint creams and which the despised acid drops?

In tactful undertones, they compared notes.

"Coo, chizz! I've got my own squashed liquorice allsort back."

"I got the toffee."

"Lucky old you. Mine was that mouldy old sticky date."

Across the room Mr Carter pulled a wry face. He hadn't inspected his sweet before popping it into his mouth and now, too late, he realised that it had a most unusual taste. It was hot on the tongue and gave off a flavour of eucalyptus. He glanced at the wrapping paper which he still had in his fingers. *Crème de Menthe*, it said . . . H'm! It tasted more like a cough lozenge to him.

Mr Wilkins, too, was puzzled. He had been eating his sweet for some minutes, and had made no impression on it. It certainly wasn't disintegrating as one might expect.

Funny, he thought! What on earth *was* this revolting confection?

By now Jennings was worried at the prodigal way in which Matron was passing the box round.

"Be careful, Matron," he advised. "There won't be any left for you if you don't watch out."

She gave him a reassuring smile. "That's all right, Jennings. You see, between you and me, I don't eat sweets."

He stared at her, appalled. "What, *never*?"

"Well, hardly ever." She noticed that he appeared to be in the grip of some strong emotion. "That doesn't mean that I'm not grateful. I'm very pleased when people give me such a nice box of – er – such a nice mixed assortment, because it means I've got some to hand round."

The room swam before Jennings' eyes. All the trouble he'd been to, and now she calmly turned round and told him that she didn't eat sweets!

"This is the second nice present I've had this term," she went on, chattily. "Martin-Jones gave me a box of peppermint creams a few weeks ago."

"Peppermint creams!"

"Yes, but I didn't eat them myself. I gave them to the boys who came up for cough medicine. They were just the thing to take the taste away."

Jennings blinked in sudden realisation. So *that* was the secret of old Darbi's private supply . . . *H'm!*

The sight of Mr Wilkins' disgruntled expression as he champed away at his long-lasting confectionery warned Jennings that it would be as well to retire to a safe distance before the situation got any worse. Matron had passed them as being tidy enough to go out with Aunt

Angela, so there was nothing to detain them in the dispensary any longer. He signalled to Darbishire who was over by the window, and they sidled quietly from the room.

Outside on the landing, he took his friend to task. "I've got a bone to pick with you! Those peppermint creams you so kindly supplied: you got them from Matron, didn't you?"

Darbishire nodded. "And what's more, I had to drink two extra doses of that ghastly cough mixture to get them – and nothing to take the taste away, either."

"But that's crazy! That means Matron's been contributing to her own present!"

"Well, why not! I knew she wouldn't mind, because she told me weeks ago that she never ate sweets, anyway."

Jennings was incensed. "Of all the double-crossing swizzlers!" he protested. "You knew that all the time, and yet you let me go to the trouble of raking up the mixed assortment."

"I did think of telling you," Darbishire confessed. "Only I thought you wouldn't be so keen to go on collecting, if you knew she'd never eat them."

"Well, of course, I wouldn't. There wouldn't have been much point, would there?"

Darbishire tut-tutted in patient resignation. "A nice mess you'd be in if I wasn't here to look after you!" he said. "You seem to have forgotten that the whole object was to stop your Aunt Angela going up the wall because you hadn't done what she told you. Thanks to me, you've got a clear conscience now – well, *almost*."

A light footstep sounded from below. Turning, they saw Aunt Angela coming up the stairs.

Miss Angela Birkinshaw, an amiable woman in her early thirties, was Jennings' favourite aunt. In his opinion she was well qualified for this important rôle, for she had the right ideas about the needs and wants of a nephew obliged to spend three-quarters of the year in the closed community of a boarding school. She was generous; she sent him parcels and postal orders when he was least expecting them; in the holidays she took him to the theatre and let him tinker with her washing-machine.

The only serious drawback about Aunt Angela was a tendency to absent-mindedness – a defect which had caused her nephew a great deal of concern in the past. On this occasion, however, she showed no signs of mental aberration: she had arrived at the right place on the right day and at the right time.

She greeted Jennings and shook hands with Darbishire whom she couldn't remember meeting before. "Perhaps I'd better have a word with Matron before we go into Dunhambury," she said to her nephew. "I'd like to thank her for looking after you while you were ill."

They retraced their steps to the dispensary. As they approached, Mr Wilkins' voice, raised in protest, could be heard booming out through the door.

"*Doh!* It's disgraceful! Why can't they label the wretched things properly! The manufacturers ought to be prosecuted – wrapping this horrible stuff up in silver paper as though it were some rare delicacy."

Jennings and Darbishire exchanged glances. "I was right," Jennings observed in a whisper. "I *thought* Old Wilkie must have picked the chewing-gum."

The protests ceased as the boys ushered the visitor into the room and introduced her to Matron and the two masters.

114

Matron thanked her for the sweets. "So kind of you, Miss Birkinshaw. As a matter of fact we've just been enjoying them." There was a mischievous gleam in her eye as she turned to her exasperated colleague. "An unexpected treat, wasn't it, Mr Wilkins! You were just remarking on their quality."

Mr Wilkins took a grip on himself and forced a sickly smile. "They were delicious, Miss Birkinshaw," he said with a gulp. "Really delicious!"

Aunt Angela had travelled by train as far as Dunhambury, and had hired a taxi for the last part of her journey to the school. The taxi was waiting to take them back to the town where a table for lunch had been reserved at the Bell Hotel; so without more ado the boys reported their impending departure to the master on duty and followed Aunt Angela outside on to the playground.

On the way to Dunhambury, Miss Birkinshaw had something to say about her nephew's progress in school.

"It was nice to get that letter from you a couple of weeks ago, but *really*, John! . . ." She sighed and shook her head. "Was that the best you could do?"

"It was a whole page, Auntie," he pointed out in defence.

"It wasn't the length; it was the appalling writing," she explained. "I could hardly read it. It looked as if a spider had popped out of the ink pot and crawled over the notepaper."

"Ah, but you haven't seen his pen," said Darbishire rushing to the support of his friend. "It's homemade. A

115

bent old crossed nib tied on to a school pencil with a bit of fuse wire. Nobody could write properly with a ghastly old relic like that."

Aunt Angela looked surprised. "Why not ask for a new one?" she demanded.

"It's Mr Wilkins' fault," Jennings told her. "Just because I happen to have lost one or two pens – well, six or seven at the outside, perhaps eight – since the beginning of term, he says I'm careless and he won't give me another one until I've found some of the old ones."

Darbishire uttered a mirthless laugh and spread out his hands in a gesture of resignation. "There you are, you see! That just *proves* Mr Wilkins is a nut-case! If Jennings could find one of his old ones, he wouldn't *need* a new one, would he!"

Miss Birkinshaw looked out of the taxi window as she weighed up the situation. Then she turned to her nephew and said, "If I were to give you a really *good* fountain pen – one that you could write nicely with – do you think you could manage to look after it?"

Jennings' eyes sparkled. "Rather! You mean with a real gold nib and a red cap and a real gold clip to fix it in your pocket with?"

"You can choose it yourself." Anything that might help to improve her nephew's handwriting was a step in the right direction, she thought.

"Coo, thanks; that's ever so good of you. We could get it in Dunhambury this afternoon, couldn't we?"

She considered for a moment and shook her head. She was thinking of the eight school penholders so carelessly mislaid. "I think you ought to do something to earn it first, otherwise you won't appreciate it," she said. "Tell me, what's your best subject in school?"

Jennings wrinkled his nose in doubt. He was near the bottom of the class in some subjects, but in others he was making good progress. Finally he said, "I was third in French in Mr Wilkins' test last week; and I would have been top if I hadn't lost marks for bad writing."

"Yes, he's ever so good, honestly. He's easily the best in the form at conversation," Darbishire said loyally. "For instance, if Mr Wilkins asks something like, '*Où est la plume de ma tante?*' Old Jennings says where it is before anybody else has even started looking."

The taxi was approaching Dunhambury when Aunt Angela gave her ruling. "Very well then, John. If you can come top of the form in French by the end of the term, you can choose the best fountain pen you can find, and I'll buy it for you."

"Thanks ever so much, Auntie. *Merci beaucoup! Très bien. Il fait beau temps!*" He beamed her a confident smile. With such a ready command of the language, the pen was as good as in his pocket already, he decided.

The taxi stopped outside the Bell Hotel where Aunt Angela paid the driver and led the way into the hotel dining-room. She chose a table by the window overlooking the car park with a distant view of the South Downs beyond.

The Bell Hotel took pride in serving homely English dishes, so the menu was not wildly exciting. Even so, it was a welcome change from school food.

"You can have tomato soup, followed by roast lamb and potatoes," Jennings announced as he studied the bill of fare. Anxious to impress Aunt Angela with his linguistic knowledge, he went on, "Of course, if it was printed in French they'd call it *potage*, followed by *mouton* and *pommes de terre*. *Mouton* means sheep really, but it's all the same when it's cooked."

He glanced across at the opposite page. "Or if you don't want that, you can have it *à la carte*. That means – er –" What exactly *did* it mean? He made a guess. "That means they bring it round on a trolley."

Darbishire nodded. "I think I'd like soup followed by sheep – er, I mean mutton – or rather lamb," he said glancing up at Aunt Angela. "At school Miss Matthews gives us ghastly old boiled beef – we call it pink hippo." He smiled apologetically. "I'm afraid I don't know how you say that in French."

The waitress took their order and returned shortly afterwards with the first course.

Jennings supped his tomato soup in silence and then glanced out of the window to admire the view. As he did so, a familiar-looking saloon car of a popular make drove on to the car park and came to rest at the far end. The driver emerged, locked the door and strode off towards the High Street with a heavy-footed tread.

Jennings watched him with mild interest. "See who's here!" he remarked.

Darbishire nodded. He, too, had recognised both the car and its driver. "Old Wilkie – er, Mr Wilkins," he translated for Aunt Angela's benefit. "The one who liked the chocolates so much. I wonder what he's doing in Dunhambury?"

Jennings shrugged. "I don't know, but it's just like him, isn't it! You'd think he'd have the decency to stay back at school on the one day in the whole term that we've got a chance to get away from him. Still, we needn't spoil our dinners by talking about old Sir all the time. It's our day off, after all!''

Chapter 12

False Alarm

As soon as the last of the boarders had departed with his parents, Mr Wilkins made his way to his garage behind the kitchen yard and set off for Dunhambury in his car. Having no duties to attend to, he had accepted an invitation to have lunch and spend the afternoon with friends who lived in the town.

He had travelled about three miles when the engine began to misbehave, propelling the car forward by fitful jerks on level ground and threatening to stall at every rising slope.

Mr Wilkins clicked his teeth with annoyance. He guessed that the cause was a worn diaphragm on the petrol pump which lately had been giving trouble and was in need of renewal. If there had been time he would have preferred to drive straight to the Star Garage in Dunhambury where he always took the car for servicing and repairs. But to do this would make him late for his lunch appointment, for the garage was on the far side of the town, a half mile walk from his host's flat in the High Street.

Mr Wilkins held strong views about guests who arrived late. Accordingly, he decided to leave the car near the town centre until after lunch and take it to the garage some time during the afternoon.

With the engine coughing and spluttering he managed to complete the journey into Dunhambury and park the car behind the Bell Hotel. He was unaware as he strode away across the car park that his presence was calling forth comment from two youthful patrons eating their lunch at the window table in the hotel dining-room.

Mr Wilkins made his way along Dunhambury High Street. As he approached the post office he saw a small breakdown lorry parked by the kerb with the words Star Garage Ltd displayed on its side. A man whom he recognised as the garage manager came out of the post office and climbed into the driving seat.

Mr Wilkins hailed him. "I say, you *are* open on Saturdays, aren't you?" he asked. "I'm hoping to bring my car in this afternoon. Spot of trouble with the diaphragm on the petrol pump."

The manager assured him that the job could be attended to without delay. "Where's the car now?" he inquired. "Brian, here –" he indicated the young mechanic in the passenger seat beside him – "he'll take it along for you if you give him the key. Save you a long walk back."

"Really! That's very kind of you." Mr Wilkins was delighted at this easy solution to his problem. He fumbled in his pocket and produced the ignition key. "It's in the car park behind the Bell Hotel."

"Righto, then, Mr Wilkins," the manager said as his mechanic climbed out and took the key. "Call in any time after four o'clock and we'll have it ready for you."

Beaming with satisfaction, Mr Wilkins strode away to meet his friends while the garage manager drove off, leaving his assistant to follow in the customer's car.

Brian Gordon Wildsmith was a young man of twenty, dressed in a leather jacket and blue jeans. He was pale

121

and thin with long black side-whiskers and a hairstyle like
an old English sheepdog. The fact that he had a somewhat
furtive manner was nothing to go by: he was a lad of noble
character and knew a great deal about cars.

He went round the corner to the Bell Hotel car park
which by this time was nearly full. When he got there he
suddenly realised one thing about cars that he *didn't* know:
he didn't know the registration number of Mr Wilkins'
vehicle!

The manager knew his customer's car by sight and had
assumed that his mechanic did, too. But now both manager
and owner had gone their ways, and there was nobody to
ask.

Although annoyed at his own lack of foresight, Brian
was not seriously perturbed. After all, he had the ignition
key: all he had to do was to find which car it belonged to.

He made his way down the line of parked cars trying
the key in the door of each one as he passed. After a
number of unsuccessful attempts he reached the last car
in the row and found that the key fitted the lock. There
was no doubt about this being the right vehicle, for a
motoring map in the dashboard pigeon-hole had the name
L. P. Wilkins written across one corner.

Satisfied, Brian Wildsmith climbed inside and started
the engine. The petrol-pump, though faulty, responded
well enough and he let in the clutch and drove out of the
car park into the High Street beyond.

He would have been surprised had he known the frenzy
of excitement that his action was causing at the window
table in the hotel dining-room.

Jennings had just finished his roast lamb when he saw
the car moving off. He leapt to his feet crying, "Hey! Stop
him, somebody! He's pinching Old Wilkie's car!"

He tried the key in the door of each car he passed.

Aunt Angela glanced at him reprovingly. "Sit down, John! Whatever's the matter? Everybody's looking at you," she said.

"But there's been a robbery. I just saw it happen. Mr Wilkins' car has been stolen."

"Nonsense," she retorted.

"Yes, honestly. Didn't you see that shifty-looking guy in a leather jacket and sideboards? He's been prowling round the car park for the last five minutes."

"*I* saw him," Darbishire said excitedly. "I was watching him. He went up to all the cars and tried them until he got to poor old Sir's; then he raced away in it before anybody could stop him."

Miss Birkinshaw looked at her lunch guests in some perplexity. She had been vaguely aware of the young man in the leather jacket moving about in the car park, but she had not paid particular attention to what he was doing. She certainly didn't know which of the cars outside belonged to Mr Wilkins; indeed, she wouldn't have noticed his arrival a quarter of an hour earlier if the boys hadn't remarked upon it. Furthermore, she didn't want to become involved in what was no concern of hers. She was enjoying her lunch and resented this disturbing interruption.

"You must have made a mistake," she suggested. "I expect the young man was just driving off in his own car."

Her nephew shook his head with the confident air of one who knows what he's talking about. He was willing to make allowances for adult ignorance but, really, her suggestion was too fatuous for words! Any boy in the school (especially Jennings) could recognise Mr Wilkins' car when he saw it.

"It *was* Mr Wilkins' car," he insisted as he sat down

again under protest. "You can't make mistakes about a thing like that. An Austin saloon with a dent in the nearside front wing."

"Registration number D 759 UKO," said Darbishire who had a photographic memory for detail where masters' cars were concerned. "And besides, we saw him getting out of it. I expect the thief saw him too; so he gave him a few minutes to get away and then – *swoosh!* and Old Wilkie's had his chips! What's he going to say when he comes back and finds it's been stolen?"

"And what's he going to say when he finds out that we saw it happen and didn't do anything about it?" Jennings said with a reproachful glance at his aunt.

Miss Birkinshaw felt troubled in her mind. The boys were so sure of their facts that she really must take some action, she thought.

The waitress was approaching to take their orders for the next course, but Miss Birkinshaw's appetite had gone. Taking a notebook from her handbag, she jotted down the make, colour and registration number of Mr Wilkins' car together with other details of identification which the boys could remember. Then she rose from the table and said, "I'll go and telephone the police. You get on with your lunch."

She was halfway across the room when she became aware that her nephew was hurrying after her. She turned to find him at her elbow with a worried look on his face. "What is it?" she asked.

"What do you want for your next course, Auntie?" Jennings inquired, as though the choice of a sweet was just as important as the theft of a car. "You can have sultana roll, rhubarb and custard, or jelly and ice-cream. The waitress wants to know."

"Order anything you like. I really don't mind," she said abstractedly.

"Or you can have cheese and biscuits, but that costs twenty pence extra."

"I'll leave it to you. Choose anything you like." Her voice took on a slight edge of impatience.

"Yes, but supposing we choose the wrong thing? Supposing we thought you'd like the jelly and ice-cream, and all the time you really wanted the rhubarb and custard!"

Miss Birkinshaw was fond of her nephew, but there were times when she found his insistence exasperating. The shock of the latest development had driven all thought of food from her mind and she was trying to rehearse what she should say to the police.

"Oh, for goodness' sake, John! Use your intelligence and don't bother me with trifles at a time like this," she said, and hurried away to the telephone in the reception hall.

Jennings returned to the window table where the waitress was still standing by to take their order. Darbishire, with his glasses pushed up on to his forehead, was studying the menu with intense concentration. Unlike Aunt Angela, the boys had no difficulty in switching their minds from one important topic to another as the occasion demanded.

"I've a good mind to have sultana roll – it's more filling," Darbishire decided after a mental tussle with himself. "What does your aunt want?"

"She wouldn't say. She doesn't want to be bothered with trifles."

"There isn't any trifle; only jelly and ice-cream. Unless, of course, she'd rather have cheese and biscuits, but I don't think it'd be fair to make her pay an extra twenty pence without asking her first, would it?"

"Oh, I don't know! I shouldn't think she'd be all that hard up."

The waitress glanced at her watch. She was a busy woman with several tables to look after.

"I think I'm going to have rhubarb and custard," Jennings said after a long pause for reflection. "It doesn't last so long as sultana roll, but it tastes better."

"M'm, yes, perhaps you're right. Perhaps I *will* have rhubarb and custard after all."

The waitress scribbled the alteration on her jotting pad.

"On the other hand, the jelly and ice-cream ought to be pretty good, provided it's not pink," Darbishire went on. "Perhaps I'll have that instead."

The waitress rolled her eyes in despair and marched off to the kitchen. If they couldn't make up their minds better than that, they could all three have jelly and ice-cream *and* like it!

While they waited for their order, Jennings stared out of the window at the scene of the crime. Presently he said, "If only I'd known in time what that guy was up to, I could have stopped him getting away."

"How?" Darbishire demanded.

"I'd have bunged a potato up the exhaust pipe. A car won't start if you do that."

His friend pondered the information. "Yes, that'd be all right if you happened to have got a spare one on you, but" – his glance flickered towards the empty vegetable dish which the waitress had left on the table. "I doubt if it would have worked with *mashed* potato though. They'd make an awful mess – especially with gravy on."

127

"I didn't *mean* mashed, you clodpoll! I meant raw ones. It was just bad luck that I hadn't got one."

"You'll know another time," Darbishire consoled him. "Never go out without a spud in your pocket in case you happen to see someone pinching a car."

It was ten minutes later that Aunt Angela returned, by which time the boys had finished their meal and the icecream on her plate was melting into a lake of tepid custard.

"Well, I've told the police," she said, as she sat down at the table. "I can't do more than that."

"What did they say?" the boys wanted to know.

"They've taken a note of the number and the other particulars you gave me so they can circulate the description; and they want Mr Wilkins to go round to the police station and take the car's registration documents so they can check up on all the details." She paused. "Now I'd like a cup of black coffee."

"Yes, but go on, Auntie; what *else*?" her nephew demanded, unwilling to be sidetracked.

"That's all! If we see Mr Wilkins when he comes back we can tell him, but there's nothing else we can do."

"But aren't the police coming round straight away looking for fingerprints and things?"

Aunt Angela shook her head. "They didn't say anything about that."

Jennings and Darbishire were bitterly disappointed. They had been hoping that the telephone call would bring a posse of police cars escorted by motor cycles hurtling through the lunch-hour traffic with sirens wailing and blue lights flashing. They could see the scene clearly in their minds' eye: policemen in flat caps cordoning off the car park, while plain-clothes detectives searched for clues and men in raincoats took photographs from every angle. Alsatians straining at the leash sniffed the ground with well-trained snuffles, and then went bounding away up the High Street with the uniformed dog-handlers clinging on to the leads for dear life! That, surely, was what *ought* to happen when somebody's car was stolen! Merely to ask the owner to stroll round to the police station with his registration documents was a pitiful anti-climax to a situation full of dramatic possibilities.

"Well, at any rate, we can be the first ones to tell him when he comes back and finds it's gone," Jennings said, trying to find some consolation for the casual manner in which the police were treating the latest criminal outrage. "I only hope he's grateful for all we've done."

They sat for some while after lunch staring out of the window in the hope of seeing Mr Wilkins return. But their vigil was in vain, and eventually Aunt Angela insisted on their accompanying her for a walk round the town to look at the shops.

This, as it happened, proved rewarding, for she bought both the boys a supply of tuck to take back to school and, in addition, Jennings found the exact model of the fountain pen that he wanted displayed in a stationer's window.

"That's the sort I'd like, Auntie! Same make, same size, same colour. I bet you what you like my writing would absolutely take your breath away if I had one of those."

"Fair enough," she agreed with a smile. "Just you come top in French and you can knock me breathless whenever you write me a letter."

After the shops, they walked across the park and then went back to the hotel for tea. There was still no sign of Mr Wilkins, so they concluded that he must have returned during their absence and made the shattering discovery of the car theft with no one present to tell him what had happened.

"How will he get back to school?" Darbishire wondered, as he sank his teeth into his third cream cake.

"By bus, of course," said Jennings, one cake ahead of his friend. "Or he may even hitch-hike. I shouldn't think he could afford a taxi if he's got to buy a new car as well."

Aunt Angela had arranged to return to London by train as soon as tea was over, leaving the boys to go back to school on the 5.25 bus. Accordingly, they accompanied her to the station, thanked her profusely for her kindness and waved till the train was out of sight.

It was growing dark as they strolled back through the town. There was a small queue waiting at the bus stop, so they joined on to the end and stood watching the traffic passing up and down, and the crowds of Saturday afternoon shoppers on the pavements.

Two minutes before the bus was due, a car came slowly along the High Street from behind them and stopped beside the tail of the queue. The driver beckoned to them, leaned over and opened the door . . .

Jennings and Darbishire stared at the vehicle in amazement. It was an Austin saloon with a dent in the nearside front wing: the registration number was D 759 UKO and the driver waving to them was none other than the legal owner, L. P. Wilkins Esq.

"I thought I recognised you two in the twilight," he called to them. "Hop in! I'll run you back to school. It'll be a lot quicker than waiting for the bus."

Chapter 13

Hold Up

Jennings and Darbishire climbed into the car seething with curiosity and surprise. So the police had been successful after all! Lucky old Sir! They were pleased for his sake and delighted at the prospect of having a sensational story to tell when they got back to school.

"So you got it back all right, then, sir!" Jennings began excitedly, as he bounced down on to his seat.

"Eh! Got *what* back?"

"Your car, sir."

"Oh yes."

No further details were offered, so after a pause Darbishire said, "Where did they find it, sir?"

"Um? Find what?" It was clear that Mr Wilkins' mind was on other matters.

"The car, sir. Did you have to go far to get it back?"

"Only to the Star Garage. It was outside on the forecourt."

"Oh!"

Still no details! It wasn't fair of Mr Wilkins to make such a secret of it, the boys thought. He must have known they were agog to hear the whole story. In an effort to draw him out Jennings said chattily, "So he didn't get very far then, did he, sir!"

Mr Wilkins frowned. What were the silly little boys talking about? Why all this interest in a perfectly normal repair job?

"*Who* didn't get very far?" he demanded.

"The man who took your car, sir."

"No; only to the Star Garage. I just told you."

This was hopeless! This was getting them nowhere!

They drove on for a few hundred yards and then Jennings said, "We actually saw him take it, sir. We saw him drive off in it."

"Saw whom?"

"The thief, sir. The man who stole your car."

"*Stole my car!*" Mr Wilkins was so surprised that he nearly passed a traffic light at red.

"Yes, sir – a crafty-looking character with hair over his eyes. Ever so suspicious, he was! He crept along like a crook and when he got to your old – er, to your car, he jumped in and raced off like lightning. We saw it all from the hotel dining-room."

"Yes, sir. And Jennings thinks he could have stopped him if it hadn't been mashed potatoes."

"What happened to the thief, sir? Did they catch him?"

Suddenly, Mr Wilkins' shoulders began to shake. He was a large man with a powerful frame, and when he saw the funny side of anything his whole body throbbed with mirth.

Seen from the rear seat, the sight of their form master's heaving shoulders was disturbing. What was the matter with the man, the boys wondered? Was he weeping? Had the shock of the afternoon's events brought on a nervous breakdown?

With an effort Mr Wilkins controlled his hilarity. "Fancy

that now!" he chuckled. "And do you know *why* you saw him driving off in my car?"

There was silence from the seats behind him.

"Because I'd just given him the ignition key. He was taking the car along to the garage to put a new diaphragm on the petrol pump."

This time there were audible gasps from the back seat passengers.

"Oh, *sir*!" Jennings' tone was resentful. He was bitterly disappointed. It was hardly playing the game, he thought, for Mr Wilkins to trot out such a simple explanation when a much more exciting alternative was available. "We were *sure* he'd stolen it, sir. In fact, we . . ."

Darbishire gave him a warning nudge with his knee. In the circumstances it might be better not to mention that they had persuaded Aunt Angela to telephone the police.

Mr Wilkins drove on towards Linbury in a light-hearted mood. Silly little boys! he thought indulgently. Trust them to get hold of the wrong end of the stick – especially Jennings! It would make an amusing story to tell Carter and the others at staff supper that evening.

He was still chuckling to himself as he drove into Linbury village and Police Constable Honeyball of the Sussex Constabulary stepped into the road, flashed a torch at the number plate and signalled the car to stop.

Puzzled, Mr Wilkins drew in to the kerb, switched off the engine and wound down the window. "Er – yes?" he queried.

PC Honeyball advanced to the offside door and said, "Good evening. May I see your driving licence, please!"

Mr Wilkins fumbled in his pocket and tut-tutted in self-reproach. "I'm afraid I haven't got it with me."

"Or the Vehicle Registration Document?"

"Sorry, no. I never carry it round with me. Why – is it important?"

The constable nodded. "I have reason to believe that the vehicle you're driving, registration number D 759 UKO was reported stolen from a car park in Dunhambury this afternoon."

Mr Wilkins stared at him in shocked surprise. "But – but – but – it *hasn't* been stolen! It's *my* car. I'm the owner."

"But you are unable to produce a driving licence. Have you any other documents to prove your identity."

"Yes – er, no. I've got plenty, of course, but not *on* me. I'm a master up at the school. You must know me by sight. I've certainly seen you about, lots of times."

PC Honeyball nodded gravely. "That may or may not be so. But as you have no proof of identity or proof of ownership, and were discovered driving a vehicle reported as stolen . . ."

"But I tell you it *isn't* stolen!" Mr Wilkins' voice was shrill with frustration. "All that happened was, I left it behind the Bell Hotel and . . ." He broke off and swung round in his seat to confront the two passengers cowering in the back. "Jennings! Darbishire! Is this your doing?" he barked. "Did *you* tell the police my car had been stolen?"

A nervous gulp sounded from behind the driver's seat and Jennings' voice came out of the gathering dusk. "Well, in a way, we did sort of mention it, but not in so many words, as you might say."

"What on earth do you mean?"

"Well, *we* didn't actually report it ourselves, sir, but we told my Aunt Angela it had been stolen, so she – well, she's very keen about people doing the right thing and helping the police, so . . ."

"*Doh!* I might have known it! You silly little boys!" Mr Wilkins stormed. "You must need your heads seeing to – especially you, Jennings!"

Jennings and Darbishire said nothing. They were hurt by Mr Wilkins' attitude. After all, they had only been doing their duty as they saw it. And supposing the car really *had* been stolen! Old Sir wouldn't be making such scathing remarks if their prompt action had put the police on the track without delay.

The exasperated owner turned back to the policeman. "You see what's happened! It's entirely the fault of these boys here," he explained. "They meant well, of course, but it's obvious that the whole thing is a false alarm." He stretched out his hand to switch on the ignition, but PC Honeyball restrained him.

"If you *don't* mind," he said in his deep, polite voice. "We'd better get this straightened out officially. If you will step into the station with me, I'll ring the sergeant in Dunhambury and get his instructions. I can't let you proceed on my own responsibility."

"Oh, but surely!" Mr Wilkins protested. "I'm in a hurry. I want to get back to school."

The policeman nodded affably. "And the only way you can be sure of doing that is by getting a certificate from me to prove you're in the clear."

"But this is ridiculous! I mean, dash it all . . ."

"Supposing you were to meet a police car between here and Linbury Court," Mr Honeyball went on in unhurried tones. "*They* wouldn't know you by sight, even if I do, and without any documents to prove who you were . . ." He drew in his breath sharply and shook his head in a way that implied spine-chilling consequences. "Better come along and get it all squared up before you find yourself in *real* trouble."

With bad grace, Mr Wilkins climbed out of the car and slammed the door loudly as a sign of his annoyance.

The police station in the village of Linbury was a detached villa of medium size occupied by PC Honeyball both as a dwelling and as a headquarters for his constabulary duties. The policeman had been standing near his garden gate when he had seen the car approaching, so the two men had not far to walk. Mr Honeyball led the way, switched on the light and ushered the unfortunate motorist into a front room which served as an office.

A few seconds later there was a pattering of youthful footwear in the hall, and Jennings and Darbishire came hesitantly into the room.

"What are you doing here? I meant you to stay in the car," the master said brusquely. "You've caused enough trouble for one day, as it is."

"Oh please, sir, can't we come in, sir? The policeman may want to ask us some questions, as we were the ones who gave the alarm in the first place," Jennings pleaded. He handed Mr Wilkins the bunch of keys that he had removed from the dashboard. "Here you are, sir! We thought we'd better lock it up in case it gets – er – so that it'll be quite safe."

In the glare of the electric light PC Honeyball could see the youthful informants more clearly. He uttered a groan of mock despair. "Oh no! Not you again! I might have known you two would have a finger in the pie somewhere." He pointed at Jennings. "Especially *you*!"

PC Honeyball uttered a groan of mock despair "Oh no! Not you again!"

For the second time that evening Jennings was shocked by the unhelpful attitude of adults who ought to have known better. He and Darbishire had both met PC Honeyball several times before, but always as public-spirited citizens bringing to his attention some information which they thought he ought to know about.* Mr Honeyball had found these encounters wearing to his nerves and patience, and the prospect of renewing old acquaintance was not one that he looked forward to with much enthusiasm.

"You might as well sit down, now you're here," he said, indicating a bench set against the wall. "It'll be warmer than waiting outside in the car." He turned to Mr Wilkins. "Shouldn't take a minute to get this straightened out. I'll just get the station officer's OK and then I can give you a form."

He picked up the telephone and dialled a number. After a short conversation he put the instrument down. "The sergeant's not available at the moment. They're going to ring back when he's free."

Ever since he had entered the police station, Mr Wilkins had been chafing with impatience to be on his way. The delay did nothing to improve his temper. "But this is ridiculous," he protested. "Why on earth the silly little boys couldn't have minded their own business . . ." He relapsed into an inaudible mumble of complaint.

They sat there for ten minutes, after which PC Honeyball tried again; but still the sergeant who was dealing with the matter was unavailable.

"This really is intolerable!" Mr Wilkins rose from his chair and paced up and down the little office. "If I'd known this was going to happen I should have . . ."

* See *Jennings' Diary*, etc.

He broke off as a thought occurred to him. He had promised to post some letters for his friends in Dunhambury on his way home, and the events of the preceding half-hour had driven this obligation from his mind. He explained his dilemma to PC Honeyball. "I've got them in the car. Do you mind if I pop out and post them while we're waiting?" he asked.

Mr Honeyball considered. "I think you'd better be here when the sergeant rings up," he said. "Just in case there's any query."

"But I shall miss the post. It goes at 6.15. And it's most important that those letters should leave tonight."

Jennings jumped to his feet. "I'll post them for you, sir," he volunteered. "I know where the box is." Anxious to make amends for his previous conduct, he stood gazing up at Mr Wilkins like a robin hoping for breadcrumbs.

The mere act of dropping a handful of letters into a post box was so simple a task that even Jennings should be able to carry out the errand without causing chaos, Mr Wilkins decided.

"All right, then. They're in the pigeon-hole on the dashboard." He tossed the car keys across the room. Jennings caught them and made for the door. "And mind you come straight back!" the master called after him as he disappeared down the garden path.

Almost immediately, the telephone rang. PC Honeyball explained the situation to his superior officer, and after a few questions replaced the receiver.

"That's all right, then. Shan't be long now," he said as he reached for a folder of official forms. "Just let me write you a certificate and you'll be on your way in two shakes of a lamb's tail."

"Thank goodness for that. This stupid business has

wasted far too much time already," Mr Wilkins grumbled.

The constable completed the form and handed it over. *This is to certify that Austin car bearing registration mark D 759 UKO, which was reported lost or stolen at Dunhambury Police Station on February 27th has been returned to L. P. Wilkins, owner, whose signature is appended*, it said.

Mr Wilkins signed the form and wished PC Honeyball good night. Then, with Darbishire trotting along behind him, he led the way back to the road.

They found Jennings waiting for them at the gate.

"Did you catch the post?" Mr Wilkins demanded.

"Oh, yes, sir. I caught the *post* all right. It doesn't go till 6.45 on Saturdays. The only thing is . . ." Jennings paused, uncertain how to proceed. It was obvious that something was weighing on his mind.

"Well, go on, boy. What is it?"

"Well, sir, something rather unfortunate happened. There were rather a lot of letters, you see, and when I dropped them into the box I was holding the car keys in the same hand and – and –" He faltered, then went on with a rush. "And by mistake I accidentally dropped the keys into the box with the letters, sir."

"You did *what*?"

Mr Wilkins performed a Morris dance of exasperation on the pavement. "*Doh!* You – you – you – silly little boy!" he stormed. "You can't be trusted to do the simplest thing. You're not fit to be allowed out! Of all the stupid, asinine things to do . . .!"

Smouldering with rage, he strode off up the road to the post box with a woebegone procession of two trailing mournfully at his heels.

There was no doubt about the time of the collection: it was 6.45 p.m. The village post office was closed, which meant that they would have half an hour to wait before the mail van arrived from Dunhambury to empty the box.

The next thirty minutes seemed the longest that Jennings and Darbishire had ever spent. There was nothing to do but stand shivering in the evening breeze listening to Mr Wilkins going on . . . and on . . . and on . . . about the idiotic behaviour of boys in general and the crass stupidity of those present, in particular.

The Post Office van arrived on time. Mr Wilkins, hoarse from nagging, explained the situation to the driver, but even then it seemed his troubles were not over.

"I can't give anything found in a post box to members of the public," the postman informed him. "Against regulations, that is. How am I to know they're really your property?"

"But of *course* they're my property! The whole thing was a stupid accident." Mr Wilkins' voice was shrill with desperation. "You don't imagine I go around dropping other people's car keys into letter-boxes just for my own selfish pleasure, do you! You don't seem to understand. I've been waiting half an hour for you to turn up."

"I understand all right," the postman returned stolidly. "What you'll have to do, mate, is to make an application in writing to the postmaster at Dunhambury stating full particulars of . . ."

"*Dunhambury! . . . In writing!*" the motorist echoed in dismay. "But that's five miles away, and anyway it's closed until Monday. I can't go on cooling my heels in the middle of the road until the beginning of next week. This is an emergency!"

The postman stroked his nose thoughtfully. "You've got a point there, mate," he agreed. "Couldn't ask anyone to hang about all that long. Wouldn't be right." He unlocked the box and fished amongst the pile of letters. Then, like an angler landing a trout, he pulled out a bunch of keys on a keyring. "There you are then!" he said, as he handed them over. "But don't you tell anybody I gave them to you. Strictly against regulations, that is!"

Mr Wilkins thanked him and then chivvied the boys back to the car at full speed.

The rest of the journey was uneventful. Mr Wilkins, frustrated and furious, didn't utter a word, his hunched shoulders clearly expressing what he thought of his passengers in the back – especially Jennings!

He turned in through the school gates, roared up the drive and stopped with a screeching of brakes outside the main entrance.

The passengers alighted. "Er – thank you for giving us a lift, sir," Jennings said politely.

"Yes, sir. Very kind of you," Darbishire mumbled.

A disgruntled "Cor!" broke from the driver's lips, and the boys fled up the steps and in through the front door, anxious to get as far away from Mr Wilkins as possible.

Mr Carter was waiting in the hall. "You're late," he told them. "You should have been back over an hour ago."

"Sorry, sir."

"Did you miss the bus?"

"Oh no, sir. We would have been back in time only Mr Wilkins gave us a lift," Jennings explained. "We've been with him ever since half past five."

"All right! Hurry up into the dining hall. Supper's nearly over."

As they scurried off down the corridor, Mr Wilkins plodded dejectedly in through the front door. There was a strained look in his eyes and he had about him the air of a man who has just passed through a harrowing ordeal.

Mr Carter nodded to his colleague and said, "It really is too bad of you, Wilkins. You shouldn't have kept those boys out so late. They look tired out – especially Jennings; and besides, they nearly missed their supper."

Mr Wilkins opened his mouth to reply and then shut it again. Mere words were inadequate to express his feelings . . . In silence he marched upstairs to his room.

Chapter 14

La Plume de sa Tante

On Monday morning when lessons started again after the half term break, Jennings settled down to work with a will. He was determined to realise his ambition to come top in French; not merely to satisfy Aunt Angela, but to prove to himself that he was capable of this achievement if he really put his mind to it.

He took a great deal of trouble in preparing some sentences for translation which Mr Wilkins set the class on Tuesday, checking them over and over again until he was sure that they contained no grammatical errors. But, unfortunately, his crossed nib played such havoc with his handwriting that the master was unable to read the finished product. Enraged at the blots and the illegible scrawl, he crossed out the whole page without correcting it and awarded the scholar nought out of twenty . . . A bad start, but worse was to follow!

For their French prep on Friday, Mr Wilkins gave Form Three a chance to use their initiative to the full. They were to draw a picture of a farmyard and prepare a list in French of the animals, agricultural appliances and anything else that they chose to portray in their scene. He was willing, he told them, to allow a fair number of marks for a good drawing; but far more important was the vocabulary which they were to learn by heart in preparation for a test on the following Monday morning.

Jennings was confident that his chance had come. He couldn't draw very well (Venables, for example, was a much better artist), but he looked forward to devoting all his time and energy to compiling a vocabulary at least three times as long and as detailed as anyone else was likely to achieve.

He set about his task with such zeal that by midday on Saturday the news of his progress was beginning to spread beyond his immediate circle.

Mr Carter heard about it during lunch. The practice at Linbury Court was for the masters to enjoy their breakfast in the comparative peace of the staff table, and to sit at the head of the boys' tables for the midday meal. By moving round at weekly intervals they were spared the nerve-racking ordeal of having to put up with the same youthful table-companions for too long at a stretch.

Presiding over Form Three table, the senior master had Jennings seated on his right and Darbishire on his left. For a time the conversation followed its usual pattern.

"Goodo! Bangers and mash," said Jennings as the first course was served. "Do you like sausage and mash, sir?"

"Yes, thank you, Jennings," Mr Carter replied.

"Do you like it as much as, say, Irish stew or curried rice, sir?"

"Yes, I think so."

"But not as much as, say, roast beef or steak and kidney, do you sir?"

Mr Carter couldn't say, not having given the matter enough serious thought.

"But surely you *must* know, sir," Jennings said reprovingly. "I know what we're going to have for every meal on every day of the week. For instance, on Mondays it's always . . ."

Mr Carter cut short the recital. "If you talked a little less about your own food, Jennings, and paid more attention to the needs of others, you might notice that I'm waiting for the mashed potatoes."

Jennings was full of apologies. "Wow! Sorry, sir, I never noticed." He called down the table to Venables who was piling potato on to his plate with the speed of a mechanical shovel loading a dumper truck. "Hey! Sir hasn't had any yet. Pass the potatoes for Sir."

From across the table Darbishire echoed the message. "Sir wants the potatoes! Pass the potatoes for Sir!"

Mr Carter raised despairing eyes to the ceiling. "*Sir* wants the potatoes," he mimicked. "Tut-tut! '*Sir*' doesn't want the potatoes."

"Don't you, sir?" said Darbishire. "But you just said you did."

Patiently, the master explained that his name was Mr Carter. "You only call masters 'Sir' when you are speaking *to* them – not when you're speaking *of* them in the third person." His audience looked vague so he went on, "For instance when I am speaking to you, *I* am the first person and *you* are the second."

"I see, sir. And I suppose Atkinson or someone is the third person if he happens to be ear-wagging in the background," Jennings deduced brightly.

"No, he'd be the fifth or sixth person because of all the other blokes in between," Darbishire suggested. He glanced down the table to where Venables was still piling vegetables on to his plate. "By the time old Ven's finished churning up the silage there won't be *enough* for a third person. They'll hardly go round another two, let alone three."

It was clear to Mr Carter that his fellow-diners had missed the grammatical point. He shook his head sadly and said, "Considering the time you spend in class learning the use of personal pronouns . . ."

"Oh, I know them in *French*, sir," Jennings broke in. "*Je, tu, il*, and all that lark. I didn't realise it was the same in English."

"Jennings is really good at French, honestly, sir," Darbishire observed. "You are, aren't you, Jen?"

"*Oui, monsieur*," said Jennings, by way of proof.

"Brilliant!" said Mr Carter. His sausages were rapidly congealing and he still hadn't got any potatoes.

"I'm hoping to come top in Mr Wilkins' test next week, sir," Jennings went on, lapsing into English for the benefit of his less learned listeners. "It's really important, too, because my aunt has promised me a terrific new fountain pen if I'm first in the class at the end of term."

Temple, seated on his right, wrinkled his nose and said, "You'll have a job to beat Venables. He's done a fabulous drawing of a farmyard – I've seen it. Not only cows and sheep and stuff, but things like combine-harvesters and fork-lift muck-rakers and all that."

"I dare say, but what's the good of drawing all those things if he doesn't know what they are in French! Ven's vocab. is hopeless!"

The artist caught the sound of his name and raised an inquiring eyebrow at the head of the table. "What's that you're saying about me?" he demanded.

"It's all right, Venables," Temple assured him. "Old Jen was just telling us he's going to get a pen from his aunt for coming top in French."

Venables grinned. "Don't talk to me about his famous aunt's feeble old pen. Sounds like Exercise 1 from some corny old textbook. 'Where is the pen of Jennings' aunt? . . . *Où est la plume de Jennings' tante?*'"

A pained expression spread over Jennings' features. He flinched and rolled his eyes in the manner of Mr Wilkins correcting an idiotic blunder in class.

"Tut-tut-tut! What a frantic bish!" he criticised in scathing tones. He turned to Mr Carter for confirmation. "There you are, sir. That *proves* Venables doesn't know any French! *Jennings' tante!* Wow! It was hopelessly wrong, wasn't it, sir!"

Mr Carter was obliged to confess that he *had* heard the French language spoken more grammatically on other occasions.

"What you *should* have said, Venables," the linguist went on in a patronising voice, "what you really *meant* was: '*Où est la plume de la tante de Jennings?*' Honestly, if you don't do better than that in the test on Monday . . ."

Mr Carter tapped him on the elbow. "Reluctant as I am to interrupt your lecture, Jennings, may I remind you that I am *still* waiting for the mashed potatoes."

"Oh, sorry, sir," Jennings apologised. He turned away and called down the table, "Potatoes, please! *Pommes de terre, s'il vous plaît! Passez les pommes de terre pour Monsieur Carter.*"

Darbishire was deeply impressed. "Wow! Did you hear that, sir!" he demanded. "Whole chunks of fluent French. Pretty good, don't you think!"

Mr Carter nodded. "*Oui*," he said, solemnly.

The first XI were playing a match that afternoon, which meant that the usual practice games were cancelled and the rest of the school were ordered to foregather on the touchline in raincoats and wellingtons to cheer the home side to victory.

Shortly before half time, Bromwich and Martin-Jones came up to Jennings, bristling with inquiry and complaint.

"Look here, what's happening about the membership club?" Bromwich began. "We know it wasn't your fault about the space-guns, but that was over a week ago. It's about time you got something else lined up, or some of us will be wanting our money back."

"And talking of money, what's happened to all our subscriptions?" Martin-Jones demanded. "Round about fifty members at five pence a time works out at something like two pounds fifty, if my arithmetic's correct."

The Treasurer, hovering close at hand, came to the Chairman's assistance. "It's all right – the money's quite safe," he assured the anxious member. "It's locked up in a toffee-tin in my tuck-box."

Martin-Jones was horrified. "In a *toffee-tin*," he echoed. "That's no place to keep vast amounts of dosh like that! Don't you know the figures for crimes of violence are going up? You can hardly open a paper without reading about smash-and-grab raids and wages being snatched left, right and centre."

Darbishire looked alarmed. The responsibility of looking after nearly two pounds fifty of other people's money had lately been causing him qualms of uneasiness whenever he thought about it. He had considered paying it into his school bank account, but hadn't dared to do so for fear it might be against the rules for boys to have control of large sums which didn't belong to them. Still, if it was a question of security, he'd have to do something about it.

"I'll see Mr Carter," he promised. "Perhaps he'll let

me open a special account so no one can accuse me of pretending it's all mine."

"Yes, but what's the money going to be spent on?" Martin-Jones persisted. "You can't just hoard it away like some gruesome old miser stuffing pound coins into an old sock – and then do nothing more about it."

Darbishire scratched his nose thoughtfully. Martin-Jones had put his finger on a flaw in the club's constitution, and before long other members would be echoing his query. Having collected the money, what on earth *were* they going to spend it on? So far, neither of the officials had been able to think of a single item that involved any outlay whatever!

He was trying to think of a face-saving excuse when Bromwich said, "I reckon the whole set-up needs looking into. Fine sort of a club this is! Rolling in money and not a single activity to show for it."

"Of course there is," Jennings countered in defence. "There's lots of things we're planning to do, actually."

"Name just *one*!"

On the spur of the moment the Chairman was unable to offer any original suggestions. "Well – er, swapping matchbox labels, for instance."

"Tut! *Matchbox labels!* If you can't think of anything better than mouldy old . . ."

"Ah, but we're doing it on a bigger scale this time," Jennings broke in, trying to devise some new variation on the old theme. "We might be having a competition – perhaps even with prizes – to see who can get the best collection in the shortest time."

The critics' suspicions were allayed – but only just!

"Well – so long as *something's* happening!" Bromwich mumbled, surly with disbelief. "But if you ask me I reckon we ought to call a general meeting of all members and get the whole business straightened out. Apart from parading around with weedy little badges, there doesn't seem to be any point in *having* a club at all."

"Hear hear!" Martin-Jones approved. He scowled suspiciously at Darbishire. "And when we *do* have this famous meeting, we'll expect a proper Treasurer's report telling us what's happening to our subscriptions – and no hanky-panky, either!"

The whistle blew for half-time and the conference on the touchline broke up. Jennings and Darbishire wandered away looking thoughtful. They hadn't realised before how serious were the responsibilities of those who volunteer to take charge of other people's money.

Jennings was at his desk five minutes before the bell rang for the end of break on Monday morning. During the weekend he had spent a great deal of time in preparing for the French test scheduled for the following lesson.

Admittedly, his drawing of the farmyard scene was no masterpiece, but to compensate for his lack of artistic skill he had managed to cram far more objects into his picture than anyone else had been able to achieve.

"And, what's more, I know what they all are in French," he informed Atkinson who had wandered up to inspect the work of scholarship. "You can test me if you like."

"No fear; that's Old Wilkie's job," Atkinson retorted. "Pretty feeble drawing, though. I can hardly tell which way up it's meant to be."

"Ah, but it's the French that matters – not the Art," Jennings explained. "I bet nobody else knows the French for a fertiliser drill or a self-propelled forage harvester."

"Do *you* know?"

"I didn't, but I do now. Mr Carter's got a French dictionary about ten feet thick and he let me look them up."

Atkinson looked critically at the crude artwork. He pointed to a cluster of improbable-looking animals in one corner. "What are these? Reindeer flying through the sky?"

"Those are cows, you clodpoll," the artist replied testily. "And they're not in the sky. They're in the distance."

"Well, if those things are meant to be cows, what are these others with television aerials sprouting out of their ears?"

"Those aren't animals at all – they're haystacks. Those handlebar things are pitchforks on the top."

Atkinson shook his head sadly as the bell rang and boys came swarming in for the next lesson. "Honestly, Jen, your drawing is chronic! You'll have to get pretty good marks for the vocab. to make up for it, or you've had your chips."

Jennings nodded abstractedly, his lips moving in a last-minute silent revision. "*Le fermier*, the farmer, *la fermière*, the farmer's wife, *la vache*, the cow, *le cochon*, the pig, *le mouton*, the sheep . . ."

He had got as far as *la charrue*, the plough, when Mr Wilkins marched into the room eager to begin the lesson.

"Come along now, you boys. Hurry up and settle down," he boomed in a voice that was audible on the floor above. "*Quietly!*" he roared as Rumbelow let his desk lid fall with a bang.

Jennings frowned at his exercise book. Would Mr Wilkins start off by marking the drawings, and then test them on the words they had used afterwards? He put up his hand to inquire.

"Put your hand down, Jennings. I'll take questions in a minute," Mr Wilkins said. "Come along now, Temple! This is no time to start sharpening your pencil. There's work to be done."

He stood frowning till the room was quiet and then went on, "Now, first of all I'm going to mark your drawings of the farmyard scene, and after that I shall test your vocabulary to see how well you've learned it!" He raised an eyebrow at the desk in the back row. "Now then, Jennings, what was your question?"

Jennings wrinkled his nose and frowned. He'd forgotten what he was going to ask.

"Well, it couldn't have been very important then," Mr Wilkins deduced. "Now, all turn to the drawings you did in prep and . . ." He broke off as Jennings' hand went up again.

"Please, sir, I've remembered my question, sir."

"What is it?"

"I was going to ask if you were going to mark our drawings first, and then test our vocab., sir."

Mr Wilkins' eyes flashed dangerously. "But I've just answered that question, you silly little boy!"

"Yes, I know, sir; only you wanted to know what I was going to ask, and you answered it before I could ask you, sir."

Pointless interruptions of this kind infuriated Mr Wilkins beyond measure. "Bring your book up to me," he barked.

Jennings trotted to the front and laid his work on the master's desk. "I'm afraid my art isn't much good, sir, but I *do* know what all the things are in French," he said with quiet confidence.

Mr Wilkins eyed the sorry-looking drawing without enthusiasm. "I can't even make out what they are in

English," he complained. "What's this splodge meant to be – a milk churn?"

"No, that's a sheep, sir – *un mouton*," the artist explained. "You can tell that because it's got legs at each corner."

Mr Wilkins sighed and awarded the drawing two marks out of twenty.

Jennings was appalled. "Oh, *sir*! Is that *all*, sir?"

"It's all it's worth," Mr Wilkins replied. "You'll have to try to catch up on the vocabulary test. I shall be giving up to eighty marks for that."

In turn, the boys took their drawings up to be inspected. Nobody else fared as badly as Jennings; most of them secured a passable ten or twelve out of twenty, and Venables, whose art was outstandingly good, was awarded nineteen marks.

Jennings wasn't unduly worried. Anyone who knew the French for fertiliser drill and forage harvester would be sure to romp home an easy winner in the final reckoning.

"Right!" said Mr Wilkins, as the last boy returned to his desk. "Now, I hope you've all got your wits about you because I'm going to test you on . . ."

The door opened and the headmaster appeared on the threshold.

"Sorry to interrupt the lesson, Mr Wilkins," he said. "Can you spare me a minute?"

"Yes, of course! Certainly."

"I'd like your opinion on those textbooks I'm thinking of ordering," Mr Pemberton-Oakes went on, as he led the way out into the corridor. "No doubt Form Three will forgive this – ah – unavoidable interruption of their studies."

Mr Wilkins smiled dutifully at the headmaster's attempt

to be jocular. Turning to the class, he called out, "Just carry on revising your vocabularies until I come back."

As the door closed behind the masters, Temple said, "Goodo! That's got rid of old Sir for a bit. Let's hope he stays out for the rest of the lesson. I expect he will, too. You know what masters are like when they get together – natter, natter, natter!"

"That'd suit me all right," said Venables. He swung round and pulled a face at Jennings in the row behind. "Two out of twenty! That's the funniest thing out! All that waffle about coming top, and all you got was a measly two."

"You wait till he tests us," Jennings replied. "I'll be laughing then. I know my vocab. backwards."

"Maybe you do, but I shouldn't try *saying* it backwards," Venables advised. "Not unless you want to put Old Wilkie into orbit."

It was nearly time for the bell when Mr Wilkins returned.

"All hard at work revising? Good!" he boomed as he strode up to the master's desk. "Now, first of all I'd better take in those marks I gave you for those drawings. I'm a bit short of French marks for this week's form order."

"But what about testing our vocab., sir?" Jennings demanded.

"I'm afraid there won't be time this lesson," the master replied as he reached for his mark book. "Not that it matters all that much. It's *doing* the work that counts, you know; not just getting marks for it."

In theory, of course, Mr Wilkins was perfectly right: there is no educational value in acquiring marks for their own sake. But on this occasion Jennings was unable to share his point of view; for, as the week's marks were taken in, it became clear that Form Three's order of merit in French was going to depend upon the results of the exercise set the previous Tuesday and the agricultural scene corrected that morning. In the former case, Jennings' painstaking effort had earned him no marks at all because Mr Wilkins couldn't read it; in the latter, his scholarly research had gained him two marks only, because he couldn't draw.

What was the use of knowing more French than anyone else, he asked himself gloomily, if the order of merit showed him to be bottom of the form? This was no way to qualify for the pen of his aunt!

Chapter 15

The Gift of Tongues

Mr Carter went upstairs to his sitting-room after breakfast on Tuesday to find Darbishire waiting for him outside the door.

"Sir, please sir, may I see you, sir? It's rather important," Darbishire greeted him.

As the master led the way into the room, his ear detected a clinking sound coming from a bulge beneath his visitor's sweater. "What can I do for you?" he asked.

The bulge disappeared as Darbishire produced a toffee-tin and laid it on the table. "It's all this money, sir. Martin-Jones says it's just asking for trouble from smash-and-grab bandits and people, even though my tuck-box *has* got a padlock." He tipped the coins on to the table. "There's two pounds forty there, sir. It should be two fifty-five, only three blokes never paid up so we crossed them off. I was wondering whether you'd look after it for me, sir."

Mr Carter agreed that the money would be safer in his charge than it would be in Darbishire's tuck-box. "Whom does it belong to?" he wanted to know.

"Well, it's like this, sir. I'm the Hon. Secretary and Treasurer of our membership club . . ."

The master nodded. He had known all about the club's

existence ever since the plastic badges had appeared on the sweaters of more than half the school. What he hadn't known about was the five pence subscription. He listened as Darbishire described the plight of a Treasurer with money to spend and nothing to spend it on.

"The space-guns were a washout, so now we've had to go back to matchbox tops," Darbishire told him. "We're doing it in a pretty big way, of course, but it still doesn't *cost* anything and some of the blokes are turning a bit nasty, sir."

"I'm not surprised. Can you blame them?"

"Well, no, not really, sir," the Treasurer admitted. "I was hoping you'd be able to suggest something we could spend it on."

"I'll give the matter some deep thought," Mr Carter promised.

"Thank you, sir. Jennings is very worried about it, too, and he's got other things on his mind as well, what with Mr Wilkins not marking the French test and everything," Darbishire went on, chattily. "He went to an awful lot of trouble learning his vocab. and now it's all wasted."

"Hardly that," Mr Carter demurred. "He can always make use of his knowledge."

Darbishire shook his head. "Not *this* time, sir! Mr Wilkins has set us a French composition now, and it's no good knowing words like haystack and cowshed and farmer's wife for an essay about a trip round the lighthouse in a rowing boat, is it, sir?"

Mention of Jennings' problems reminded Mr Carter of a matter he had been meaning to investigate earlier. "You went out with Jennings' aunt at half term," he remarked. "Have you written to thank her?"

Darbishire's hand flew to his mouth in guilty realisation.

"Well, no, sir, I haven't actually quite finished the letter yet," he confessed, meaning that he hadn't actually quite started it yet, either.

"Very bad manners on your part! Go and write it now. You've just got time before assembly."

"Yes, sir." Darbishire picked up his empty toffee-tin and turned to go. A box of matches on the mantelpiece caught his eye. "Oh, sir, may I have that matchbox, please?"

There was no need for Mr Carter to ask why. The revival of interest in collecting matchbox labels as a membership club project had meant that for the past few days masters had been walking around with their pockets full of loose matches with no box to strike them on.

He nodded his assent, and then exclaimed, "Hey! Leave the matches behind! I only meant you could have the lid."

He sat down at the table and began collecting up the coins as the door closed behind his visitor. Two pounds forty was a worthwhile sum of money, he reflected. He'd have to make sure that it was put to good use.

Downstairs in the common room, Darbishire got out his writing pad and began his letter.

How should he start, he wondered? She wasn't *his* Aunt Angela, and *Dear Miss Birkinshaw* sounded absurdly formal considering they were on such friendly terms. He compromised and wrote: ·

Dear Aunt Birkinshaw,
    Thank you for taking me out with Jennings (*i.e. viz.* John) at half term. I enjoyed it very much also the jelly and ice-cream it was very good even though it was pink. The car was not stolen he had gone to a

garage for a new thing and he gave us a lift to school but it took a long time to get to school.

What else could he say? There was the fountain pen, of course. Poor old Jen didn't look like getting it if things went on as they were shaping at the moment. Perhaps he could put in a good word on his friend's behalf. He continued:

Jennings (*i.e. viz.* John) has not come top because of his writing which Mr Wilkins crosses out and does not read because of his pen, so how will he do now we have got a French essay round the lighthouse in a rowing boat if he won't even read it let alone give him any marks because it is only a homemade one and makes blots all over the place. Thank you for taking me out I enjoyed it very much.

Yours,

(singed) C. E. J. Darbishire.

On Friday it rained hard all morning; and though the sun came out after lunch, games were cancelled as the pitches were too wet for football. Instead, the boys were sent out into the school grounds in wellingtons and sweaters to work off their surplus energy in the open air before afternoon school.

Jennings and Darbishire scampered around with their friends for some while, and then wandered down to the main gate to watch the cars going past. Although, technically, it was a main road, there was seldom much flow of traffic past the school gates, and the only vehicle in sight when they arrived was a grey car parked by the verge some twenty yards down the road.

It is doubtful whether they would have given it a second glance but for the fact that it had a foreign index number and a plate marked with a capital *F* on the rear wing. There was no driver, but a boy of about their own age, wearing a yellow anorak, was sitting in the front passenger seat.

"French car," said Jennings, stating the obvious. An idea skidded across the surface of his mind. "I wonder if they've got any French matchboxes they don't want."

Darbishire's eyes sparkled at the prospect. "Wow! That'd be a real scoop, wouldn't it! Old Venables and Co. would be green with envy if we got hold of a whole new batch of foreign ones." He glanced again at the Gallic appearance of the boy in the passenger seat. "Bags you do the asking."

"Why me?"

"Well, supposing he doesn't speak English," Darbishire argued. "You'll have to tell him that you don't want the matches, only the box. Or rather, not even the box – just the lid. And then you'll have to explain that you'll give him another lid in exchange for him to strike the matches on."

"Phew! All that in French?"

"Yes, of course."

There was a pause. Then: "Let's not bother, shall we! Perhaps he hasn't got any matchboxes, anyway."

Darbishire snorted in derision. "Well, I like that! All that waffle about coming top in French! All that gefuffle about being awarded the *plume* of your famous *tante* . . ."

"All right, all right, I'll have a bash," Jennings put in hastily. "I'll have to work it out first, though." He narrowed his brows in thought. "I think I'll start off with: 'Good day! It is very fine today, is it not?'"

161

"No, it isn't. It's as wet as a shower bath."

"Oh, shut up, Darbi. The point is, I know how to say that: *il fait beau temps*. And after that – oh, fish-hooks! What on earth's the French for doing a matchbox swap?"

Darbishire grinned. "I shouldn't worry. It'll probably come to you when you get going."

With some misgiving, Jennings led the way to the parked car and smiled at the youthful occupant through the window. The boy smiled back and opened the door, but said nothing.

"Good afternoon! I mean, *bonjour*," Jennings began. "*Il fait beau* – er, I suppose you don't happen to speak English by any chance?"

The boy looked at him without understanding and said: "*Je ne parle pas anglais. Il faudra que vous attendiez que mon père revienne. Il est allé téléphoner à un garage, car la voiture ne marche pas.*"

Jennings was out of his depth. "Oh goodness! I beg your pardon?" he queried.

The boy got out of the car, tapped the bonnet and shrugged. "*La voiture: elle ne marche pas.*"

Ah yes, of course! *La voiture*, the car, Jennings reasoned. But surely *marcher* meant to walk?

"What does he say?" Darbishire demanded.

"He says the car won't walk."

"Won't *walk*!" Darbishire echoed in surprise. "But surely . . ."

"Stop nattering, Darbi! I've got enough on my plate coping with this bloke in French without you gibbering in English at the same time."

From his pocket Jennings produced a matchbox label and held it out. Hesitantly he began: "Look – er – *regardez! Avez-vous* any matchbox tops *pour* swapper *avec moi?*"

Though the idiom was faulty, the meaning was clear enough to break through the language barrier. The French boy opened his eyes wide in sudden understanding. "*Ah oui, bien sûr,*" he said. "*Vous voulez échanger des boîtes d'allumettes avec moi. J'en fais collection, moi aussi. Je vais vous montrer.*"

He hurried round to the boot of the car and reappeared shortly afterwards with a handful of French matchbox labels. Eagerly he exclaimed: "*J'en ai à peu près cinquante. Si vous en avez des anglaises, j'aimerais bien les échanger.*"

Jennings was delighted. Here, obviously, was a keen collector.

"What did he say then?" Darbishire wanted to know.

"He said how about swapping some of his for some of ours."

Darbishire was impressed. "He said all that! And you actually understood every word."

"I didn't go by the words. I went by the look on his face," Jennings explained. He flicked through the foreign matchbox labels and his face creased in a triumphant smile. If they could effect an exchange with the French boy their own collection would be the envy of the membership club. The best plan would be to take him – and his labels – indoors where he could inspect their collection and make his choice of "swaps".

It was not easy to explain all this in French, but by the aid of gesture, mime and a great deal of pointing, Jennings managed to convey the invitation to their new companion.

The French boy appeared willing to go with them, though on one point he expressed some anxiety. "*Est-ce qu'il y en aura pour longtemps?*" he demanded. "*Mon père va revenir dans quelques minutes.*"

This was too difficult for Jennings, but even so his guess

was fairly near the mark. "Something about his father," he translated. "Still, we shan't be keeping him long, so I expect it'll be all right."

As they made their way up the drive Darbishire felt inspired to try his skill at conversation in a foreign tongue. After racking his brains for some moments in silent rehearsal (My name is Darbishire. What is yours?), he took the plunge and said: "*Je m'appelle Darbishire et mon ami* – this bloke here – *s'appelle Jennings*. What is *votre nom?*"

To his surprise the French boy appeared to understand. "*Je m'appelle Henri Dufour*," he replied. "*Je suis venu ici avec mon père, car il veut m'envoyer en classe en Angleterre.*"

Darbishire nodded. "You don't say! Well, fancy that now!"

"Fancy *what*?" Jennings demanded.

"I don't know, but it sounded pretty important. The only bit I got was that his name was Henri something."

When they reached the top of the drive they met Venables and Temple who stared at their companion with curious interest.

"Hullo, who's this guy?" Venables demanded.

"He's a friend of ours. His name's Henri," Jennings explained. He pulled a face at Venables. "It wouldn't be any good *you* trying to talk to him because he doesn't speak English, and everyone knows your French is just too pathetic for words. *I* get on with him all right, though."

Venables accepted the insult without comment. "Yes, but what's he doing here?" he wanted to know.

"We're just taking him indoors to . . ." Jennings stopped abruptly. To reveal that the pockets of Henri's anorak were filled with exciting foreign matchbox labels, which he was anxious to exchange, would. bring every collector in the membership club running to take part in the bargaining. The market would be swamped; rare labels would be snatched up before the Chairman and Secretary had had a chance to make their own choice. No, this was a case where the organisers were entitled to priority. After all, whose idea was it?

"We're going to do a spot of private business," Jennings went on. "I can't tell you more at the moment because it's a secret. You'll know all about it in time, though."

So saying, he took his guest by the elbow and steered him across the playground towards the side door.

165

Chapter 16

The Fellow-Phillumenist

Venables and Temple exchanged puzzled glances as the trio disappeared into the building.

"Sounds fishy to me! Distinctly fishy," Venables observed. "There's something going on that we don't know about."

"I'd like to know what it is too," said Temple. "It doesn't make sense on the face of it. It isn't even as though they could both speak the same language."

They turned the problem over in their minds as they continued their aimless saunter down the drive. As they reached the gate, Venables stopped in his tracks and smote his brow in sudden realisation.

"Wow! Petrified paint-pots! I've got it," he cried.

His companion raised an inquiring eyebrow.

"I've solved their guilty secret . . . That boy speaks French!"

Temple nodded. "So what? If he comes from France you wouldn't expect him to talk in Icelandic, would you!"

"No, but don't you see! He'd be the very bloke to help you write a French compo about going round the lighthouse in a rowing boat."

There was a short silence while Temple considered the evidence. Then he said, "Yes, of course. It all fits! Ever since Jen came bottom last week he's been telling everyone he was going to make up for it."

"So what does he do!" Venables demanded dramatically. "He gets hold of this guy to write his compo for him in perfect French and, hey presto, he's top of the form."

"Crafty!" said Temple.

"It's more than crafty – it's cribbing. It's downright dishonest! It'll serve him right if Old Wilkie rumbles it."

From where they were standing they could see a grey car with a French number plate parked beside the verge. Now, however, it was not the only vehicle in sight, for a mini-van inscribed Star Garage Ltd was drawn up in the road behind it. The bonnet of the French car was raised and a young man in blue jeans, with black sidewhiskers and a chrysanthemum hairstyle was carrying out some roadside repairs. Standing nearby was a tall, middle-aged man who appeared to be the owner of the car.

As the boys watched, the mechanic finished his task, lowered the bonnet and then ran the engine for some moments to prove that all was well. Satisfied, he exchanged a few words with the motorist who produced a wallet and paid for the work which had just been done.

Then, as Brian Wildsmith drove off towards Dunhambury in his van, the middle-aged motorist looked up and down the road in some perplexity. Catching sight of Venables and Temple he waved to them and made his way up to the gate.

"Excuse me, I have lost my son," he said with an unmistakable French accent. "Have you seen a boy aged twelve years? He is wearing a yellow anorak. I am concerned because he does not speak English."

Venables and Temple were only too willing to be of assistance. "We know where he is. He's just gone into our school," Temple explained. "If you'll come with us, we'll try to find him for you."

"Thank you. You are very kind," said the motorist. "I did not know there was a school here. I shall be interested to see your school and perhaps I shall meet your teacher, also."

Venables couldn't imagine why any right-minded tourist should want to spoil his holiday by hobnobbing with English schoolmasters, but it wasn't his business so he made no comment. Instead he led the way up the drive, assuring the bereft father that his son would be restored to him without undue delay.

The boys escorted Monsieur Dufour to the library and then went off to begin their search. This proved more difficult than they had expected, for there was no sign of the guest in any of the rooms they visited. There was no sign of Jennings and Darbishire either, even though they extended their search to include such unlikely places as the shoe-room and the bicycle shed.

One place where it *didn't* occur to them to look was the boiler room at the far end of the basement . . . Here, behind the bolted door, three keen phillumenists were happily bartering matchbox labels in sign language, safe from invasion by others of their tribe.

At the end of twenty minutes Temple said, "This is hopeless. There isn't a whisker of them anywhere. What on earth's his father going to say?"

"I reckon we'll have to tell one of the masters and get them to deal with it," Venables replied. "Mind you, it'll mean trouble for Jennings if we do, but there's nothing else for it."

They retraced their steps to the front hall where they met Mr Carter and Mr Wilkins coming out of the dining hall.

"Sir, please sir, we've put a French gentleman in the library," Venables announced. "He's looking for his son, but there's no sign of him."

"He must have come to the wrong place," said Mr Carter. "Didn't you tell him we haven't got any French boys here?"

Venables shook his head. "Actually we *have* got one at the moment – we met him on the playground. Jennings and Darbishire were looking after him, but now all three of them have disappeared."

Mr Wilkins snorted. "They're a fine pair to look after anyone – especially Jennings! I wouldn't leave those two in charge of a stuffed mule, let alone a live French boy. When I think of all the trouble that boy Jennings has . . ."

His colleague interrupted to say that Jennings' short-comings were of less importance at the moment than the whereabouts of the missing visitor. "I'll go along to the library and see the father," he said. "He may be able to shed some light on the mystery."

"He won't be able to help you, sir," said Venables. "*He* doesn't know why his son went off with Jennings and, of course, we didn't like to tell him."

Mr Wilkins stared at him in suspicion. "So you *do* know what's behind all this, Venables!"

"Well, sir . . ."

"Come along now, out with it. What's been going on?"

Venables and Temple looked uneasy. They had no wish to land Jennings in further trouble, but with Mr Wilkins standing there glowering at them and demanding an answer, what else could they do?

"Well, sir, I don't like to tell you really, because it's

sneaking," Venables began unwillingly. "But Jennings is very anxious to come top because he's been promised the pen of his aunt, sir."

Mr Wilkins was baffled. "What has the pen of Jennings' aunt got to do with his inviting a French boy into the school?" he demanded.

"Everything, really, sir. You see, you set us a French essay about going round the lighthouse in a rowing boat and . . ."

Light dawned in Mr Wilkins' brain. "Doh! So that's the game, is it!" he exclaimed. "Passing off as his own work an essay in French written by a native."

"Oh no, this boy isn't a native, sir. He hasn't got a tom-tom or anything like that."

"A native of *France*, you silly little boy!"

"Oh, sorry, sir."

"Tut! Just wait till I see that boy Jennings again!" the master went on in tones suggesting that he had just unmasked the most infamous fraud of the twentieth century. He turned to see how his colleague was reacting to the news of the villainy, but Mr Carter had already departed to the library to reassure Monsieur Dufour that the question of his son's whereabouts was now officially in hand.

Temple and Venables were about to resume their search when the latter happened to glance out of the window. . . . Crossing the playground were the three missing phillumenists.

"There they are, sir!" he cried. "They're taking him back to his car at the end of the drive!"

"Run and stop them," Mr Wilkins ordered. "Take that French boy along to the library. Tell him his father's waiting for him."

"Yes, sir," Venables turned to obey and then stopped short. "How *can* I tell him though, sir? I don't think my French is good enough for that."

Temple gave his friend a scornful look. "Better get old Jennings to help you out then," he suggested. "*He* seems to get on all right in French, even if he *is* bottom of the form."

The four o'clock bell was ringing for afternoon school as the boys scampered off on their errand. Mr Wilkins stood watching from the window as, somehow or other, his instructions were conveyed to the visitor who was then led off towards the library. In the wake of the escort party, Jennings and Darbishire trotted back into the building to get ready for the first lesson.

Mr Wilkins frowned. He'd have something to say to Master Jennings before the day was over!

There was a rumble like distant thunder as seventy-nine dining-hall chairs scraped along the floorboards and the school rose from the tables at the end of tea.

Shortly afterwards a knock sounded on the staff-room door, and Jennings appeared on the threshold in response to Mr Wilkins' booming invitation to "Come in".

"Please, sir, you sent for me, sir?" Jennings' manner was relaxed and he spoke in tones of polite inquiry. He had nothing on his conscience – well, not more than usual – and he couldn't think why the master was looking at him with such a forbidding expression.

Mr Wilkins said, "Come in and shut the door," but there was a lack of warmth in the invitation. He sounded like a potato-farmer welcoming a Colorado beetle. "You don't deny, I suppose, that you asked that French boy into

171

the school this afternoon and went to some pains to conceal his presence?"

"We didn't actually *hide* him, sir." Jennings' expression was all wide-eyed innocence. "We only bolted ourselves in the boiler room because we didn't want everyone to know what he'd come for."

"*That* I can well believe! And what makes it worse is that, even now, you show no signs of shame for your disgraceful behaviour – stooping to an act of deception to gain marks dishonestly."

Jennings stared at him in bewilderment. What on earth was the man talking about? "I don't understand, sir."

"Oh yes, you do! You brought that boy in specially to help you with your French essay."

"Oh, but I *didn't*, sir." Jennings was shocked at the charge, but Mr Wilkins, bristling with indignation, gave him no chance to explain.

"Never in all my life have I come across such an outrageous case of cheating. You're a disgrace to the form, Jennings – a disgrace to the school!"

It was at that moment that Mr Carter came into the room. Unaware of the lecture in progress, he extended a friendly nod in the boy's direction and said, "Ah, I see you've got Jennings with you. I've just been hearing glowing reports about him."

Mr Wilkins paused in his tirade. "Glowing reports? From whom, may I ask?"

"From the headmaster. He's delighted with the initiative Jennings and Darbishire showed this afternoon."

There was something wrong somewhere, Mr Wilkins decided. This just didn't make sense. "You mean to say the headmaster *approves* of boys smuggling foreigners into the school to write their essays for them!"

"Oh, but, sir, I never did . . ."

"Be quiet, Jennings! Venables and Temple were in no doubt as to what he'd come for."

"But they didn't *know*," Jennings persisted. "We didn't let them into the secret."

"Now we're coming to it," said Mr Wilkins. "So there *was* a secret."

"Yes, sir. Darbishire and I asked him in to show him our matchbox top swaps."

Mr Wilkins' eyes opened wide and his jaw dropped. "M-m-m-match-swap-box-tops!" he echoed, inaccurately.

"Yes, sir. He'd got some rare foreign ones, and Darbishire and I are collecting for our membership club project, you see."

"That's quite right," Mr Carter confirmed. "I heard all about it when I took Henri and his father along to meet the headmaster. There was nothing sinister about his activities in the boiler room: it was merely that he was a fellow-phillumenist."

"Oh, I don't think he's *that*, sir," said Jennings. "He told me he came from Normandy."

Mr Carter sighed. "A phillumenist, Jennings, is the name given to a person who collects matchbox labels."

Jennings looked surprised. "Honestly, sir? Wow! I've been doing it for terms and I never knew I was one of those before."

Mr Wilkins listened with growing bewilderment. It *still* didn't make sense to him. "Yes, yes, yes, but why the glowing reports?" he queried. "You don't mean to tell me that the headmaster considers exchanging matchboxes is a sign of great initiative!"

"Good gracious no! It wasn't that at all," Mr Carter explained. "But it was all due to Jennings that Henri and his father came in. Monsieur Dufour is looking for an English school for his son, and now he's seen Linbury he's decided to send him here as a boarder."

There was a pause while Mr Wilkins digested the information. Then he said, "I see! Very well then, Jennings, we'll say no more about it. I'm sorry I jumped to the wrong conclusion."

"That's all right, sir," Jennings assured him. It was not often that he had the satisfaction of receiving an apology from his form master. He gave him a kindly, tolerant smile to convey that even though Mr Wilkins might not have a forgiving nature he, J. C. T. Jennings, was prepared to adopt a more enlightened outlook in matters of this kind. . . . But Mr Carter's next words wiped the kindly smile from his lips.

"Henri doesn't speak English at the moment, but the Head thinks that if we do our best to help him, he should be able to manage the work in Form Three," he said.

The room swam before Jennings' eyes and his hand shot to his mouth in a gesture of horrified dismay. "Oh, *no*!" he gasped. "Not in *my* form, *please*!"

"Why not?" queried Mr Carter. "I should have thought you would have been delighted, considering that you were the first to make friends with him."

"Yes, but don't you *see*, sir," Jennings cried. "I've been working my best ever since half term specially so that I can come first in the class."

"A very worthwhile ambition," Mr Wilkins approved.

Jennings flipped his fingers with exasperation. "Yes, but

I've gone and bished it all up now, sir," he said bitterly. "And it's all my own fault . . . How on earth am I ever going to come top of the form in French if we've got a genuine French boy in the class?"

Chapter 17

Account Rendered

As the days passed, the seeds of mistrust sown by Bromwich and Martin-Jones gave rise to fantastic rumours about the fate of the Jennings Membership Club subscriptions. Various theories were put forward to prove that the funds had been either (a) lost, (b) stolen, (c) confiscated, (d) hidden up a drainpipe, (e) buried under a compost heap, or (f) squandered by the officials in pursuit of their own selfish pleasure.

"I'm tired of telling everyone the money's quite safe," the Treasurer confided to the Chairman as they were getting ready for bed on Tuesday evening. "I wish now we'd never agreed to *have* subscriptions at all."

"That was *your* idea," Jennings reminded him. "You were so keen to go prancing around with an account book sticking out of your pocket that you wouldn't listen when I said there probably wouldn't *be* any expenses anyway." He wrinkled his nose in thought as he screwed up his dressing-gown into a tight ball and stuffed it into his clothes locker. "Still, that isn't going to help us at the meeting. We've just *got* to think of something sensible to spend the money on."

It was this meeting, demanded by the members and fixed for the following evening after prep, that was causing the Chairman and Secretary some concern. They had at their disposal the considerable sum of two pounds forty and, as yet, not even the ghost of a notion as to how it could be spent to advantage.

Mr Carter was on dormitory duty that evening; and when he came round to put out the light, Darbishire reminded him of the promise he had made the previous week.

"You said you'd try to think what we could do with the dosh, sir."

"The *what*?"

"Sorry, sir – the money, I should say. Have you had a chance to think yet, because I've got to make my Treasurer's report at this meeting tomorrow and it may be a bit – well, I'm hoping it'll go off all right, sir."

Mr Carter smiled. "It's not so easy being a Treasurer, is it! Especially of a club that was in such a hurry to get going that it couldn't wait to decide what its aims and objects were!" He pondered for a moment and said, "I can think of one suggestion, but of course it would be up to the members to decide for themselves, and as I'm not a member of the club . . ."

"Oh, but you *could* be, sir," Jennings broke in eagerly. "An honorary member: not even five pence to pay. And then you could come to the meeting and make suggestions."

"That'd be terrific," the Treasurer agreed. "We've still got some badges left – members have to wear them, you see, to prove who they are."

"Never mind the badge. I think most people in the school know me by sight," Mr Carter said gravely. "If not, the Chairman will have to introduce me."

The two boys felt a little easier in their minds as they

settled down to sleep. They were not out of the wood yet, but at least they had an ally on whose advice they could rely.

The next morning Jennings received an unexpected letter from Aunt Angela. He opened the envelope at the breakfast table and found a postal order attached to the sheet of notepaper inside.

"What's all this in aid of?" he exclaimed in puzzled wonder. He ran his eye down the page and then turned on Darbishire accusingly. "Hey! You never told me you'd written to my Aunt Angela!"

"Just an ordinary thank-you letter for taking me out at half-term," his friend assured him.

"Well, you certainly rang the bell as far as she was concerned. She says here you told her I hadn't got a chance of getting any marks until Mr Wilkins could read my writing."

"Some sort of flannel like that," Darbishire agreed. "I can't remember exactly; it's so long ago."

"Well, anyway, she thinks you're right, so she's sent me the money to get the pen straight away. Terrific of her, isn't it!"

With his spoon, Darbishire transformed the mountain of cereals on his plate into a volcano with a crater going down the middle. "The only snag is you haven't got an excuse for *not* coming top, once you've bought a proper pen; and with old Henri what's-his-name in the same class . . ."

"You needn't bother about him," Atkinson put in from across the table. "He's not coming 'till next term. Mr Carter said so."

"Honestly?" Jennings' eyes lit up with renewed hope. There were still three weeks to go before the end of the term. Aided by legible handwriting and with foreign competition out of the running, he still had the chance to prove to Aunt Angela that her trust had not been misplaced.

John Christopher Timothy Jennings was a boy of determined character. More often than not he set his sights too high and missed his target altogether, but on this occasion he proved as good as his word. On the last day of term Mr Wilkins had to total the score in his mark book three times before he could bring himself to believe that he had not made a mistake. . . . But there was no miscalculation. Jennings had come top in French!

Meanwhile, however, Jennings had other things to worry about; and the chief of these was what was going to happen when the Membership Club foregathered after prep to hear the Treasurer's report. True, Mr Carter had hinted at having some vague proposal up his sleeve, but Jennings was inclined to treat this with caution. He knew from past experience that grown-ups had peculiar ideas about the ways in which money ought to be spent. He passed a restless day brooding over his problems, and it was almost a relief when the bell rang for the end of prep and members wearing little badges assembled in the common room to air their views and defend their rights.

The meeting was well attended. Although many of the members had lost interest in the club after the space-gun fiasco, they turned up that evening in strength hoping for sensational developments and anxious to be in at the kill if charges of gross mismanagement could be proved against the club officials.

The first item on the agenda was the Treasurer's report. To be on the safe side, Darbishire had withdrawn the club funds from the school bank and brought the whole amount along to the meeting in case of argument. His toffee-tin half full of coins lay on the table before him as, notebook in hand, he stood up, coughed nervously and read the statement of accounts . . . *Cash received, two pounds, forty . . . Expenses, nil . . . Balance in hand, two pounds, forty. . . .*

In the back row Binns and Blotwell checked the Treasurer's arithmetic on the backs of old envelopes. They were unable to find any flaw in his reckoning.

The Chairman rose as the Treasurer sat down.

"This proves that the money hasn't been wasted on a lot of extravagant expenses," he began. "The next thing to decide is what we're going to do with it. Any suggestions?"

Martin-Jones jumped to his feet. "Money back!" he demanded in a truculent voice. "It's our rhino by rights, so the only fair thing is to pay everybody his five pence back again."

There were murmurs of assent.

"Any other brainwaves?" the Chairman asked.

"Yes, I've got a better scheme," said Temple. "Let's spend it all on a feast, and have a whacking great slap-up blow-out. For two-forty we could get some doughnuts and fizzy drinks and stuff." His eyes sparkled at the prospect. "That's what I vote, anyway."

Temple's proposal was well received in various parts of the room; informal arguments broke out about the choice of menu, and grew louder and louder until the Chairman called the meeting to order.

"That's two ideas," Jennings announced. "We'll have to take a vote on it unless anyone else has got something sensible to put forward."

There was silence for some moments while the members racked their brains for further suggestions. When it was clear that nobody else had anything to propose, Mr Carter rose to his feet. He had slipped into the room just after the meeting started and had remained almost unnoticed in the back row while the discussion had been going on.

"We've had two proposals put forward," he began. "Both of them are feasible, yet they both involve frittering away a sum of money which could surely be put to better use. The whole purpose of any club is that the members combine to achieve a worthwhile result in some field of activity. The trouble with *this* club – if you'll excuse some blunt speaking from the newest member – is that so far it hasn't made up its mind what sort of a club it's meant to be and what sort of a goal it's aiming at."

The members sat up and took notice. Mr Carter had certainly made a point.

"Everybody here in this room is fortunate in that he lives in a country in which a decent standard of living is accepted as natural," the speaker went on. "Your welfare in such matters as health, food and education is never for a moment in doubt. But what about boys and girls in less developed countries who are deprived of the things which you take for granted? I don't have to tell you that in other parts of the world young people of your age are suffering from hunger and disease, and will never have the opportunities which you have of learning to read and write and developing the full use of their minds.

"We can help them if we want to. There are societies dealing with famine relief and the welfare of deprived boys and girls who are desperately in need of every penny they can lay their hands on!"

Mr Carter paused and glanced down at the sea of faces looking up at him. They were quiet now, and attentive:

the whole atmosphere of the meeting had undergone a change while he had been speaking.

"Well, there you are," he said in matter-of-fact tones. "If you want your money back or decide to spend it on pop and doughnuts, that's entirely up to you. On the other hand, if this club is trying to find a worthwhile reason for its existence, you might like to consider my suggestion." He glanced at his watch. "Twenty-to-eight! You'll have to excuse me, Mr Chairman. I'm late for an appointment with the headmaster."

There was silence for some moments after Mr Carter had left the room. Then Martin-Jones lumbered his way up to the officials' table.

"Money back?" inquired Jennings. He held out five pence in coppers but Martin-Jones shook his head, fumbled in his pocket and dropped two coins into the toffee-tin.

Temple followed hard on his heels. He turned his trouser pockets inside out and produced three pennies and a second-class postage stamp which he deposited on the table. Then he turned and addressed the meeting.

"Listen!" he said. "You can scrub what I said just now about having a blow-out. We don't do too badly compared with some people – even on school cooking."

The meeting had closed and the members had dispersed when Mr Carter looked into the common room on his way back from the headmaster's study twenty minutes later.

The Chairman and the Secretary, however, were still there sorting out copper, silver, and postage stamps and stacking them in neat little piles.

"Situation under control?" Mr Carter inquired.

They nodded, smiling.

"How many wanted their money back?"

"Nobody, sir."

"Really! And no votes for what was delicately described as a whacking great slap-up blow-out?"

"Oh *no*, sir. After what you said, Temple threatened to bash up anyone who seconded his proposal," Jennings informed him. "Not that anyone wanted to. They all voted for the money to go for famine relief."

Mr Carter nodded. "Splendid! So you've got the whole two pounds forty to devote to a very worthy cause!"

The Treasurer looked quietly amused. "No, not two-forty, sir – eight *pounds*. After you'd gone the meeting voted to treble the subscription, and the extra eighty *p* is a sort of backwash from *la plume de la tante de Jennings*, as you might say – at least it *will* be, when he gets change."

"He means my aunt, sir," Jennings explained. "She sent me the money to buy a fountain pen, and I happen to know you can get a cheaper one: it's just as good for writing with, only not so much gold and stuff on the cap. So I thought – well, I thought – after all, I thought – what's eighty *p*, I thought, so . . ."

He seemed slightly embarrassed and unable to bring his sentence to a close. Tactfully, Mr Carter butted in and said, "That was generous of you, Jennings; and what's more you'll have the satisfaction of knowing that even if the Membership Club did nothing else in its short life, it justified its existence when it finally wound up its financial affairs."

He stopped, aware that both boys were staring at him in shocked surprise.

"Oh, but, sir, the club isn't *packing up*," Darbishire protested. "Just the opposite! We've decided to go on raising funds for famine relief, as our chief project."

"Yes, sir, and there's all sorts of ways we're planning to do it, now we know what the club's really *for*," Jennings maintained. "For instance, we're going to . . ."

The dormitory bell shrilled out its bedtime summons and Mr Carter raised a hand to stem the flood of suggestions.

"Tomorrow," he said firmly. "It's too late to discuss important matters at this time of night."

"Yes, sir . . . All right, sir . . . Good night, sir!"

"Good night, Jennings; good night, Darbishire."

The two scurried away to their dormitory leaving Mr Carter to cope with the coins and the toffee-tin.

He watched them go with mixed feelings. On the one hand he was delighted that the Membership Club had at last found a worthwhile objective: with Jennings in charge the club would no doubt muddle its way through to the goal it had set out to reach. On the other hand, the project could well leave in its wake a trail of chaos and confusion that set Mr Carter's orderly mind boggling with apprehension.

That was the trouble with boys like Venables and Temple and Darbishire and Jennings, the master reflected as he scooped the coins back into the toffee-tin. Their intentions were excellent: they had the right ideas. . . . But they just *didn't* know when to stop – especially Jennings!